SHADOW IN THE DARK

For Samwise
always loved

Shadow in the Dark

The Harwood Mysteries

Book 1

Antony Barone Kolenc

Loyola Press.
Chicago

LOYOLA PRESS.

3441 N. Ashland Avenue
Chicago, Illinois 60657
(800) 621-1008
www.loyolapress.com

Cover art credit: Martin Beckett, MahirAtes/iStockphoto/Getty Images.
p. vii-ix Map art credit: Martin Beckett
p. vii Map insert, Floorplan of an Abbey: Kathryn Seckman Kirsch
Back cover author photo: SSSPHOTOGRAPHIC, LLC

ISBN: 978-0-8294-4810-8
Library of Congress Control Number: 2020930779

Printed in the United States of America.
20 21 22 23 24 25 26 27 28 29 Lake Book 10 9 8 7 6 5 4 3 2 1

Contents

How to Read Historical Fiction

Shadow in the Dark is a work of historical fiction. This type of book differs from nonfiction because the story is imagined by the author and does more than simply tell you "what happened." Rather, this type of book helps you, the reader, understand what happened in history while drawing you in and entertaining you. The story invites you to make connections with situations and characters and to discover what stays the same for people of any period and also determine what might have changed over time.

Even though the characters and events are imagined, an author of historical fiction tries to be accurate when presenting what it might have been like for a specific group of people to live and work in a particular time and place. That's why an author might present scenes and dialogue that differ greatly from what we experience today.

These differences are also why some of what you read might feel foreign or even shocking. As you read, remember that in some cases, the characters aren't doing something "wrong"; they are simply doing what was considered acceptable at that time. As the reader, it's important for you to read critically throughout. If you're interested in learning more about the historical context of *Shadow in the Dark*, you'll find more information in the back of the book, in the Author's Historical Note.

Here are some tips for making the most of *Shadow in the Dark*.

Before Reading

Do some brief internet research about life in 12th-century England and in a typical abbey of that time. Watch a video, view illustrations, or read an article to gain some historical context.

During Reading

Ask yourself questions such as the following:

- In what ways are children's everyday lives the same in the Middle Ages when compared to yours? In what ways are they different?
- In what ways are the actions and reactions of young characters like those of kids today? In what ways are they different?
- God and religion played a significant role in the lives of people during the Middle Ages. In terms of God and religion, how are the characters' thoughts, words, and actions like the people of today? How are they different?
- How have society's expectations for girls changed over the centuries?

After Reading

Ask yourself questions such as the following:

- What ways of thinking or acting do you see as consistent for people no matter the time period? What ways of thinking or acting are different now? In each case, do you think our new way of thinking or acting is better or worse? Why?
- This book often references the idea of "God's will," a common concept in the Middle Ages. What have you been taught about this concept? What are your thoughts?
- In the feudal system of the Middle Ages, serfs and laborers were considered to be of less value than people in other stations in life. Where do we see examples of this today? How might societies be able to correct these injustices?

GRENTON PRIORY

PENWOOD MANOR

OAKWOOD MANOR

LUCY'S MANOR

HARWOOD ABBEY

ROMAN ROAD

Floorplan of an Abbey

1. Church
2. Cloister
3. Kitchen and refectory
4. Scriptorium
5. Dormitory and infirmary
6. Confinement cell
7. Lavatory
8. Chapter house
9. Library
10. Garden
11. Cellar
12. Abbot's house

Tragedy

T he boy jolted awake to a thunderous drumming. He rolled off his straw mattress. The dirt floor trembled beneath his toes, almost tickling them. *Da-doom, da-doom, da-doom.*

"Father? Mother?"

Vapor puffed from his mouth in the dim light. Dawn must be near.

Across the cottage, Father sprang to his feet, his thick hair jutting out in all directions. "Listen. Horses!" He pulled a brown tunic over his head as Mother stirred next to him.

The boy grabbed his own tunic, sticking his arms into its scratchy woolen holes. Then he slipped on a pair of thin leather shoes. Father might need his help.

Hoots and curses and screams rang out from the far side of the village—a chaotic mix of angry shouts and terrified cries. Hardonbury Manor must be under attack!

Mother clung to Father's hand, her eyes wide with fear. "What do we do, Nicholas?"

"Stay here!" Father bolted out the crooked wooden door, letting in a rush of misty air.

Bitter smoke stuck to the boy's tongue—not the pleasant smell of the hearth, where Mother heated their broth each morning. Nay, it was foul smoke, worse than the stench of the fire that had burned the crops in the West Field last year.

Mother sunk her face into her hands.

"Don't worry." The boy hugged her tight. "God will protect us."

"Son!" Father's voice called from outside.

"Coming, Father!" He squeezed Mother's hand and burst out the flimsy door.

A surge of heat slapped his face as flames sprang up from the thatched roof of a nearby cottage. The manor house on the hill was burning, too! Dark clouds of smoke poured from windows on its high stony walls—like rows of filthy chimneys staining the red sky of dawn.

Villagers scurried about in all directions, but six burly men had gathered to defend Hardonbury with their tools: hoes, shovels, and long scythe blades for the wheat harvest.

Father stood among the defenders, taller than the rest. His shoulders were squared, and his eyes glistened in the firelight. Maybe Father wanted him to join the battle.

"I'm here, Father."

"Nay! Take Mother and run, son," Father yelled. "'Tis bandits!"

Just then, the village blacksmith sprinted down the lane toward them, his huge hands balled into fists, pumping back and forth. A bandit dressed in black pursued him on a sweaty horse. Dust swirled into the smoky air with the strike of each hoof.

The horseman held a long wooden mace crowned with metal studs. He bore a jagged scar on his cheek, and his thick, crooked nose looked as though it had been broken and never healed. He kicked the blacksmith to the dirt, then swung the mace and hit the poor man's head with a bone-cracking blow.

"Get ready, men!" Father said. He waved his son off: "Not you."

The boy shook his head hard. He would never run and leave Father to fight alone. He might be only eleven years old, but he'd worked the fields with Father each day and cleaned the tools with Father each night. He was old enough to fight bandits with Father, too.

Five men on horseback rode up in a cloud of dust, joining the scarred bandit. They circled the defenders, penning the boy out. A few of them carried crossbows fitted with sharp quarrels. He couldn't get to Father without fighting through them. More bandits were heading this way, too, judging by the sound of it.

"What'a we do with this bunch, Rummy?" a pig-eyed bandit asked the man with the scar.

Rummy lifted the bloody mace in his fist and peered down at Father and the others. "Drop your weapons now or we kill you all."

The boy reached to the ground and picked up a stone. A short, thin bandit sat upon a brown horse nearby. If he could hit that bandit with a stone, it might create an opening, and he could run to help Father inside the circle, where an extra shovel lay on the dirt.

As the boy took aim, a child cried out in terror from the cottage across the path—the voice of little Alden, only six years old. The child's cottage was on fire!

Alden's father was standing with the other men, and his mother and sister had died last year in the plague. That meant Alden was all alone as the flames on the roof rose higher.

There was no one else close enough to help the child.

The boy dropped his stone on the path. "I'll be right back, Father!"

He ran to the burning cottage. Alden was pulling desperately on the jammed door.

"Stand back, Alden!"

He kicked the door hard with his heel, splintering its frame. Shards of wood hung limply as the door fell to the dirt. The child raced out, his face streaked with mud and tears.

"Alden, run to the East Field!" he said. "Someone will get you soon."

The child nodded and ran toward the East Field.

The boy headed back to Father and the others, who were holding their tools high toward the bandits, ready for battle.

"We will never give in to you," Father told Rummy. The others shouted in agreement.

"As you wish," Rummy said. He gestured to his men. "Kill them."

The boy picked up the stone again. He needed to be at Father's side for this battle, but his delay in helping Alden had stolen his only chance.

"Halt!" a tall bandit commanded, entering the circle from the lane on horseback. This one seemed to be their leader. He wore a chain-mail shirt, and his face was lined with deep, curved creases that faded into a silver beard on a pointed chin. A pendant hung around his neck on a thin rope—a carved wooden star and, at its center, a dragon with jewel-green eyes.

"Carlo." Rummy drew his horse aside. "We were just taking care of these troublemakers."

Carlo groaned. "I weary of your needless killing," he said. His voice almost sounded sad.

"Ach, you are getting too old for this." Rummy spit on the dirt. "Leave the killing to me."

The boy shifted his arm and took aim at Rummy, who would be the greatest threat to Father.

Carlo sat up straight in his saddle and grabbed the hilt of his broad, iron sword. He thrust it toward Rummy's throat. The boy might not need to hit Rummy after all.

Carlo held the sword higher and pointed it toward the manor house, still burning on the hill. "Our mission is done. Why are you wasting time on these peasants?"

Rummy laughed. "The men are excited. They want a little fun."

Carlo scowled at him under his wrinkled brow. "You set fire to the whole village!"

"What does it matter?" Rummy said.

"Can you not follow simple orders?" Carlo pulled the reins on his horse and rode slowly from the circle. "Now, gather the men and follow me."

The village might be saved after all. There would be fires to put out and injuries to heal, but the bandits' attack would soon be over.

But as soon as Carlo had left the circle, Rummy stared down at Father, who still held tightly to a shovel, his eyes defiant.

"I will at least teach *this* one a lesson." Rummy raised his mace into the air. With it he could crush Father's head, as he'd done to that poor blacksmith.

"Nay!" The boy threw the stone with all his might. It struck Rummy in the center of his ugly nose, sending him flying off his saddle to the dirt with a thud and a grunt.

The boy cheered, along with some of the villagers. Even a few of the bandits laughed as Rummy rolled to his feet with mud stuck to the top of his nose.

Suddenly the boy's face grew cold. Rummy was charging at him, waving his mace with wild eyes that streamed with furious tears. "You will die for that, boy!"

"Run!" Father yelled, as the other bandits closed ranks around the defenders.

He ran. He raced down the side lane that led to the East Field, glancing back only once. Rummy was gaining on him. He passed cottages on both sides, many of them still burning. No one was around. Maybe they'd fled, or the bandits might have killed them all.

He chanced another look. Rummy was nearly upon him, cursing and spitting as he came.

Finally he reached the East Field, where a few rows of golden wheat stalks remained standing in the midst of the harvest. A wooden bucket hung from a post: drinking water for the field laborers.

He grabbed hold of the bucket and swung it behind him. He released it.

"Ahh!"

He looked back. Rummy, drenched with water, had stumbled over the bucket. Now there'd be a chance to put some distance between them.

He crossed the field and headed toward the thick trees. That would be his only hope of escape. If he could get to the woodland trail, he could outrun the tiring bandit in the forest.

Then what? The trail would lead him to Harwood Abbey. The monks there might protect him or at least send word to King Henry that bandits were raiding the countryside. Then he could circle back home and help Mother and Father with the repairs.

"Stop!" Rummy shouted behind him.

Why wouldn't the bandit give up the chase? That stone must have hurt more than just his nose; his reputation with the other bandits might be at risk. They'd laughed at him.

The boy kept running. He could work the fields for hours at a time without a break under the glare of the withering sun. Surely he could run a half hour to save his life. Yet after a while the green branches passed more slowly, some scratching at his arms as the trail narrowed.

Rummy's curses followed him. "You cannot . . . run . . . forever!" The bandit must be near exhaustion by now.

The trail opened to its widest point, with a clear path to Harwood Abbey.

His woolen tunic clung to the sweat on his back despite the frosty morning air. Pain in his side—cramping muscles pleading for a break. Nay. Rummy was still pursuing.

Suddenly his foot hit something, and he plunged to the dirt with a yelp.

The tree's thick root—stretching across the trail—shouldn't have surprised him. He'd bounded over roots like that before, pretending they were serpents waiting to strike his heel.

"Get up, you simpkin!" he said to himself, brushing a wet flop of hair from his forehead. Blood seeped from scrapes on his knees and palms, yet he pressed his hands to the dirt.

Rummy sprang upon him from between two trees, tackling him back to the ground.

The bandit seized his ankle—he couldn't get back on his feet now. He kicked and hollered, but Rummy's icy grip seemed unbreakable.

"Now die, boy!"

Lord, save me!

Rummy growled and raised the mace high to strike him.

Darkness. Then, out of darkness came piercing, bright light. Just for a moment.

Dizziness. Darkness again.

Rough arms under his legs and around his back. Bobbing back and forth.

He opened his eyes, but the light punished him, jabbing behind his brow with daggers. Whoever carried him was dressed all in black.

Nausea in the pit of his stomach. Darkness again.

How much time had gone by? Someone still carried him.

He chanced another painful glance. No more; it hurt too much.

Whoever held him was wearing a black robe; carrying a long, thin pole.

Dizziness. Nausea. Everything swirling in darkness.

Black robe? Maybe this was the angel of death, coming to take him to the netherworld.

He opened his mouth to speak, but only a wrenching sound and vomit came out.

Then a long darkness.

Memory

T he boy's foot was stuck in a hole, cold dirt all around it.

A slender trail stretched before and behind him. Trees with dying leaves and sharp branches jutted at him from the sides of the path, their points sticking like thorns every time he moved.

Why couldn't he get his foot out? And how had he got it stuck to begin with?

The brush rustled on the other side of the trail. Footsteps crunched dead leaves.

"Get out of there!" he yelled at his trapped leg. Something was coming.

A black, hairy boar-like creature crept from between two trees—eyes speckled with blood, snout crooked and covered in mud, and fangs dripping with spit. It stared at him as though it starved for his flesh. It would eat him here, stuck in this hole in the middle of nowhere.

Unless he could defend himself. He looked for a stone to throw. A big round one was just within reach. He grabbed it, raised it high. The creature scurried off.

Too easy. Had he really frightened it with a stone? Nay, something else had scared it.

There—down the trail coming toward him—a giant figure in a black robe that dragged along the earth. Skeletal hands stuck out from its dark sleeves, but a draping hood shadowed its face. It held a long, thin scythe blade in its bony right hand. The ground shook as it walked.

This must be the angel of death, coming to take him down to the netherworld.

Someone once said that if the angel of death embraced you, it would take your soul. Who told him that? It didn't matter. He was going to die now, or he might be dead already.

Still, he couldn't get his foot out of the hole.

He shut his eyes tight. "Nay!" he shouted. "I don't want to go with you!"

"Wake up," a voice said. The angel of death's voice was soft, almost gentle.

Hands grabbed his shoulders. This must be it—Death's fatal embrace.

"Wake up," it said again.

He opened his eyes.

A black robe leaned over him; hands held him firmly by both shoulders. He pushed hard against the robe. "I don't want to die!"

But as he pressed into the angel of death, his hands touched tenderness, not bone. The black robe retreated from him, taking two steps back, as though it had been startled.

He closed his eyes and opened them again. This wasn't right at all.

The trees were gone. The trail was gone. The hole was gone.

He wasn't on hard dirt; this was soft cloth. He lay in a bed.

How had he got out of the forest and into this little room? Light gleamed through a narrow window in a stone wall. A wooden desk stood in a corner with a tiny stool.

There was no hideous creature, no angel of death—only two men next to the bed. They wore black robes with long, hooded cowls.

Sleeveless vests draped over their robes, and belts encircled their waists.

They gaped at him and at each other.

Maybe it had all been a nightmare.

The younger man—the one he'd pushed away—leaned a bit closer to speak. He was thin and clean-shaven, but his eyes were different colors: one brown and one blue.

"I am Brother Andrew," he said in the angel's gentle voice. "Be at peace, my son."

The man bowed in a gracious gesture, revealing a head shaved in the style of a tonsure, with a large bald area on top and a narrow ring of hair encircling it. Someone had once told him why some men shaved their heads this way. If only he could remember the reason or who had explained it to him.

"We are Benedictine monks," said the older man, who stroked a well-groomed white beard. A large belly pushed out his robe in the center. "You are recovering in the infirmary here at Harwood Abbey. I am Father Clement, the prior of this abbey—second only to the abbot himself."

Harwood Abbey. That name sounded familiar. He might have been here before.

He tilted his head to take in the whole room, but pain shot across the back of his neck. What was wrapped around his skull? He reached to touch his hair only to find cloth bandages. Something must have happened to his head. And that nasty smell in the air must be his own stench. How long had he been stuck in this bed? And how had he gotten here?

The monk with different-colored eyes—Brother Andrew—nodded. "Aye. You were injured, child. Do you remember?"

The hole; the creature; the angel. Nothing else. He shook his head just barely.

The monk seemed disappointed. "No matter," he said, patting the boy's arm.

"What are you called, boy?" the prior asked. "Your name?"

He cleared his throat to speak, but his voice still croaked out like dust. "I am called . . ."

What *was* he called? The question was simple enough. Everyone had a name.

"I am called . . ."

The monks exchanged a glance.

"Do not worry, boy; you are probably just famished." The prior patted his own generous belly. "You have been recovering here four days. Do you wish for something to eat?"

He gave a pained nod, though his growling stomach had already given the answer.

"I will go fetch you something," the prior said, stepping from the room.

That left Brother Andrew, who pulled the stool next to the bed and sat, smoothing out the wrinkles on his robe. It was long and dark, like the robe of the angel of death.

The boy's face tingled and grew cold.

"Do not be frightened," the monk said, looking intently at him. "All Benedictine monks wear black robes. 'Tis why they call us the 'black monks,' you know."

He must have been staring too hard at the monk's robe.

"There are also the 'white monks' of Citeaux; they wear white robes." The monk gave a mischievous wink. "Our robes are better than theirs."

He forced a smile for the man, who was trying so hard to cheer him up. The monk must feel sorry for him, lying with bandages on his head, not even able to remember his own name.

The prior returned with a wooden tray. On it was a small wood plate and cup that held beans, a loaf of dark bread, and some water.

"Take, eat," the monk said.

He sat up. Dizziness. He paused a moment before speaking. "Thank you."

He attempted a few bites of the dry bread, but chewing caused pain to shoot up his cheeks. The bread could barely get moist enough to swallow. He took a sip of water, joyously wet and sweet. He started eating faster, and Brother Andrew started talking faster.

"No doubt, you have heard of Saint Benedict. He was the founder of our community over six hundred years ago. He wrote *The Rule* that governs our lives."

This time the monk said it as though he didn't expect an answer.

It was one thing not to know about the monks' founder and all their rules. Why would he know any of that anyway? But surely he must know something about his *own* life.

Like his family—everyone had a family, so where was his? Did he have a brother, or sister? That seemed something a person should know. In fact, how could he know what a "brother" or "sister" was, yet not remember whether he had one or the other?

He ate another bit of bread that he'd rolled and softened between his fingers.

He must have a mother and father. Where were they? Did they know he was at this place?

He finished his last sip of water.

Brother Andrew spoke again. "My son, do you remember your name now that you have eaten?"

He shook his head.

"How about the name of our king, boy?" the prior said. "Or the year?"

"The king." He paused. The king ruled the land, of course. "His name is King . . ."

When he didn't continue, the prior said, "'Tis Henry, son of the Empress Matilda."

"And 'tis 1184, of course," Brother Andrew added, with an encouraging smile.

The boy shrugged. None of these were supposed to be tough questions. Something must be very wrong with him. He'd been seriously hurt, but how and where and why?

"Please," he said. "Do you know anything about me at all?" This talking had made his head pound with pain, his temples stabbing at his forehead on both sides.

The monks exchanged another glance. They seemed worried.

"Nay," Brother Andrew said. "The abbot—our leader—is very old but very wise. He thinks you might be from Hardonbury Manor. 'Til today, we had three days of rain. Perhaps the storms have kept your parents from coming for you."

He'd been at the abbey for four days, and the monks still hadn't found his parents. Even with rainy weather, that seemed a long time for his parents not to come.

"What is the last thing you remember, boy?" the prior asked.

He thought hard before answering, so hard that his head could burst. "I . . . I was dreaming."

"Aye, we heard you cry out," Brother Andrew said.

"I . . . I was stuck in the woodland. Then . . . then I woke up here. But how did I get here?"

"We found you in the woodland," said the prior. "It seems you have lost your memory."

That made sense in some way. "But how? Will I ever get it back?"

"I have seen such a case once," the prior said. "At my first monastery we had a monk who fell down the well and banged his head. He still knew all our prayers, but he had no idea how he had become a monk or where he had grown up. 'Twas a strange situation indeed."

Maybe that's what happened. He'd banged his head in the woodland and now could only remember general things about the world but nothing specific about himself.

"Did the monk ever get his memories back?" he asked.

The prior nodded. "Eventually, after about a year. They came back all at once to him in a painful flash of light, he told me."

He gasped. "A year?" Even without his memory he knew a year was a long time.

"By Adam, that is not good," said Brother Andrew, his blue eye glistening in the window-light brighter than his brown one. "This poor lad cannot go about being called 'boy' for a year."

The monk sounded as though he expected him to be at the abbey a long time. Had they already given up on finding his parents? They must know something they hadn't told him.

The prior nodded. "Of course not, Andrew. You shall give him a name for now. And you shall tend to his needs, too."

The younger monk stood. "But I have my prayers, Father Clement. And my work in the scriptorium. And my duties as an obedientiary. Will he not stay in the dormitory with those other poor lads—the ones who came to us after the plague last year?"

"Have faith, Andrew. Am I not prior? The boy will move to the dormitory soon enough."

The prior took the boy's hand. "I must leave now—I am a priest and must go ready myself to say Mass. Brother Andrew will answer all your questions. And you shall have a marvelous name, I am certain."

But he already had a name. Surely his parents would be upset if he started calling himself something new. He wasn't a stray dog, to be renamed by everyone who happened upon him.

Still, he squeezed the prior's hand and tried to sound grateful. "Thank you, Prior."

The older monk departed, leaving Brother Andrew staring out the slit window.

The monk might be upset about caring for him. It seemed he was going to be a burden on these poor monks until his parents found him—*if* they ever found him.

Suddenly Brother Andrew turned back to the bed with a wide smile. "I have got it!" He snapped his fingers. "Your name, I mean."

His head throbbed worse than ever, and the dizziness had returned. Plus, he didn't know any names, so how would he know if the monk was going to give him a good name or a bad one?

Brother Andrew sat back on the stool. "You are a hearty lad. You have battled well against a serious injury to your head these past four days. I believe I have a fitting name for you."

Hopefully the monk wasn't going to name him Hard Head or Strong Boy or anything like that.

"Alexander." Brother Andrew suggested the name simply, with no explanation.

"Alexander," the boy muttered.

Alexander.

Pressed down by a great weight of fatigue, he allowed his head to fall back on the mattress and let the darkness come again.

Xan

He opened his eyes to sunlight streaming through the infirmary window. He was alone.

Thump, thump, thump, thump, thump. A constant hammering of wood upon stone sounded through the slit—workers threshing wheat in the distance.

"Wait," he said aloud. "How do you know they're threshing wheat, Alexander?" He said his new name again very slowly. "Al-ex-an-der." Such a long name. What did it mean?

He pulled his hands out from under the warm scratchy blanket and looked at them in the chill light. There were callouses on his fingers and around the edges of his palms. He'd probably worked the fields and threshed wheat back in Hardonbury.

His parents could tell him when they came for him. The sooner they found him, the sooner he could stop being a burden to Brother Andrew. Then the monk could get back to his praying.

His stomach rumbled. "Time to get up, Alexander," he said.

A clean brown tunic lay folded on the stool. Next to it was a white rope and a leather pouch.

He kicked off his blankets and sat up. *Ouch!* He needed to go slower than that to stop the pain from clobbering his head. He gingerly swung his feet over the bed into warm, morning light.

Taking tentative steps, he reached for the tunic and inched it over his head, careful not to disturb the bandages. Then he tied the rope and pouch around his waist. The monks also had left him leather shoes under the bed. He slipped them on, steadied himself, and headed for the door.

He collided with a coarse black robe.

"Trying to walk about alone, you foolish child? You are scarcely healed."

The hard eyes of an elderly monk stared down at him, gray eyebrows sticking out from his forehead in unexpected ways. The man seemed familiar, yet certainly he hadn't visited the infirmary last night. The monk pointed a thick, purply finger in the boy's face.

"Were you not told you are forbidden to walk alone in the monks' dormitory?"

Why was this monk so angry? The others had been so nice. "I was just—I wanted—I . . ."

"Speak quickly, child." The monk's ancient face could not tame the fire burning in his eyes. He resembled the others: a tonsured ring of silver hair, a flowing black robe and cowl, and a sleeveless vest worn over top. Except the other monks had been patient and gentle.

"I . . . I'm hungry."

"And I am Brother Leo." The monk stepped out of the room.

He didn't move. What did the man expect him to do?

Brother Leo glared back at him. "By Peter's staff, I do not have all day. Follow me, boy."

He hurried behind the old mean monk, who led him past a small supply room and into a long hall with narrow wooden doors all shut tightly. Dark-colored paintings decked the walls. In one, a bright-eyed soldier with a broad sword and a cross in his belt marched toward a walled city—so joyful for war.

Brother Leo stopped abruptly and turned, pointing to one of the little doors.

"These hallways are forbidden to you, boy. These are the monks' cells."

That didn't sound like a place any monk would want to be. "Prison cells?" he asked.

Brother Leo threw his thick hands into the air and huffed. He pressed down the handle on one of the doors. It glided open with a creaking sound. "What does this look like to you, child?"

Inside the empty room, a lonely bed with a thin straw mattress butted against a bare stone wall. A tiny desk and slender wood chair stood in the corner. On the far wall hung a wooden crucifix with the body of Jesus carved upon it. On the bed was a long, thin, wooden pole.

"It looks like a place to sleep."

"This is my cell," Brother Leo said, not quite meanly. "In some abbeys, the monks sleep in rows of beds in a common room. Not here. We rest and pray in our own cells."

He pulled the door closed with an echoing slam and kept walking.

All that slamming and reprimanding had brought a throb back to Alexander's head, but he continued to follow the monk closely through the labyrinth of hallways until they reached a larger door. The monk opened it and they stepped outside into cooler air. Birds chirped all around. The blazing sun pierced through branches of a tall oak, inflaming his headache even more.

They strode along a cobblestone path, past a lofty stone building with ivy growing up its sides. Finally they passed under a tall door into a dining hall. Empty wooden tables and benches lined the floor, and paintings hung on high walls of stone. Small windows allowed the daylight to invade, but the spacious area was grayer and dimmer than the infirmary.

"Wait here in the refectory," Brother Leo ordered, as he marched back outside.

He plopped down on one of the benches. What was he supposed to be waiting for? And what was a refectory?

Maybe someone would bring him more bread. Or his parents might have arrived and were coming to meet him here. Unless they'd abandoned him. Or worse.

The monks were not telling him everything—that was certain. It could not be an everyday occurrence for a boy to wake at an abbey with a serious head injury and no parents. Surely boys didn't just stray into the woods and lose their memories. How had he banged his head?

For a moment, an image flashed into his mind. The woodland. Smoke. Something held him in its arms. A black robe. The angel of death? Nay, he hadn't died. A monk then, carrying him to the abbey. But which monk? Unless it all had been a dream.

Someone started sweeping outside the refectory. Moments later, the door burst open.

A red-haired boy entered, as short and slim as the broom clenched between his dirty fingers. The child continued to sweep but finally spotted him sitting on the bench. The boy—eyes growing wide on his freckled face—glanced in both directions before creeping to the table.

"Is everything all right?" he asked the child.

"I'm Joshua." The boy spoke in a low voice, as though he were doing something wrong.

It was nice finally to meet someone who wasn't wearing a black robe. This must be one of the boys Brother Andrew had mentioned, who had come to the abbey after a plague.

"Hello, Joshua." Maybe he should have introduced himself to the boy as Alexander. Or it might be better to wait until he learned his real name.

He must have spoken too loudly because Joshua glanced back at the door and then stuck a crusty finger to his thin chapped lips. "Did you see anything last night?"

"See anything? Like what?"

Joshua's voice dropped to a whisper. "The Shadow."

"See a shadow?"

"Aye, on the fields at night. 'Tis coming to take our souls."

"Like the angel of death?"

Joshua dropped the broom to the floor. "So you *did* see it!"

He'd seen it all right—in his first and only memory before waking up here at this abbey. This poor little boy might have had a similar nightmare with no one there to comfort him.

"Everyone has bad dreams sometimes," he said gently to Joshua, the way his own mother might have consoled him as a child.

The boy picked up the broom with a stomp. "Nay! Not a dream; it was real."

Dreams could seem real. The angel of death that had haunted his own dream had felt real enough, but trying to explain all that to Joshua would probably insult the boy. It wasn't his job to mother Joshua—he had his own family to find. But who else would help the poor child?

"How old are you?" he said.

Joshua's eyes grew indignant. "I'm not a baby. I'm almost nine years old, and I'm not the only one who saw the Shadow. David and John have seen it, too, and they're almost twelve."

So maybe it wasn't a dream then. Perhaps a misunderstanding?

"I believe you, Joshua. You've all seen this shadow, but has it taken anyone's soul yet?"

Joshua's eyes shot left and right, perhaps to ensure the Shadow wasn't eavesdropping on their conversation. "Well, actually, on this one night when—"

The door to the refectory swung open; the startled child yelped.

Brother Andrew entered with a smile, followed by a tall, slim man with a bushy mustache that curled around the edges of his lips. The other man wore a brown tunic, much like his own, and carried a wooden tray holding a cup, a head of cabbage, and a black loaf of bread.

"Good dawning, Alexander," the monk said. "I see you have met one of our fine lads."

Joshua squeezed the broom and started sweeping again. "'Twas just working my chores, Brother." The child scurried out the door.

The man with the brown tunic placed the tray on the table, bowed to Brother Andrew, and exited without a word. No black robe—that might mean the man wasn't a monk and that other kinds of people also lived at the abbey.

"How are you feeling this morning, Alexander?" Brother Andrew asked.

Alexander put a hand on his bandages and winced. "I think I'm well enough to go find my parents." He bit into the bread loaf, which crumbled around his lips.

Brother Andrew reached out and pulled on the bandages.

Ouch! Though the monk grasped them gently, each tug caused a sharp pain until the final bandage fell to the stone floor.

"There. How is that?" Brother Andrew said.

The pounding had already begun to lessen, as though his head was joyously celebrating its freedom from bondage. "A bit better, thank you."

"Excellent." Brother Andrew smiled. "Last night, while you slept, the abbey's leech examined you and said your bandages could be removed today."

Maybe the monk was playing a joke on him. Leeches were slimy little creatures that lived in rivers. How did he know that, anyhow? Perhaps he had seen one, or his parents had told him.

He smirked at the monk. "A leech really told you that, Brother?"

The monk's laughter echoed through the high-ceilinged room. "Not an actual leech, my son. A 'leech' is a monk learned in herbs and medicine who uses leeches for healing."

How odd.

He bit into the green cabbage, so moist that it squirted water on his tongue while he chewed.

"As for your parents," the monk said, "I have no news to report. But I have spoken with the prior and the abbot about your situation, and we have come up with a plan."

Five days without his parents coming could mean they didn't want to find him for some reason. Unless they didn't know about Harwood Abbey. "Is Hardonbury far? Can I go there?"

The monk shook his head. "Far, but not too far. Today, the plan is to get you settled and give your body a little longer to heal. Tomorrow, the abbot directs me to take you to Hardonbury."

He frowned. Another day without knowing his parents or his real name.

"All right, Brother. If you think that is best."

"Now tell me," Brother Andrew said. "How do you like the name I have chosen for you?"

Alexander. Surely that wasn't the name his parents would have given him, so long and difficult to say. Yet the monk had been delighted by it.

Brother Andrew must have sensed his doubts. "Your namesake is Alexander the Great, one of the great warriors of history. Over a thousand years ago, his father, King Philip of Macedon, conquered Greece and built an empire. While still a boy, Alexander showed courage, strength, and great wisdom. He was tutored by none other than Aristotle, the brilliant Greek philosopher."

The monk must be quite a dreamer to give such a name to an injured boy who threshed wheat. Brother Andrew's face lit up as though he'd fought alongside Alexander the Great himself.

"Alexander the Great led his army on a crusade that captured many lands. My son, you should have seen it—soldiers as strong and numerous as the sands of the Sahara. All feared them. And at only nineteen years, that boy ruled one of the greatest empires this world has ever known."

The monk patted him on the shoulder. "That is why I chose the name Alexander. I sense there is more to you than meets the eye."

The name had dignity—maybe too much dignity. Falling down in the forest and banging your head didn't make someone worthy of such a name. Unless the monks knew he'd done something strong and courageous in the forest and were keeping secrets from him.

"Do you not like the name?" Brother Andrew's expression sank in disappointment.

He shrugged. "'Tis a fine name, Brother. Except . . . 'tis so long to say."

The monk smiled. "I can solve that. What if we called you Xan for short?" He pronounced the nickname as "Zan."

Much shorter and simpler, even a bit mysterious. *Xan*—the boy with no name and no memory. The look on his face must have provided all the answer Brother Andrew needed.

The monk clapped his hands. "'Tis settled, then. Now rise and follow me, Xan. 'Tis time you met the other boys and moved into the dormitory."

No doubt, some of the boys were older than Joshua. They'd probably make fun of him: a new boy with a made-up name and no memory. What would he have done back in Hardonbury if boys had made fun of him? He might have cussed or punched them. Or would he have run away?

Brother Andrew was still talking. "First, I will introduce you to the monk in charge of the boys. Since the plague, a few of our monks have taken turns each week watching over the dorm."

"And whose turn is it this week?" Xan asked.

"Brother Leo."

That was the mean old monk. Brother Leo would probably be sticking his fat finger into Xan's face a lot, screaming at him to hurry up and do chores.

"Why do you make a face?" Brother Andrew said, staring at him. "Brother Leo is a good man." The monk ushered Xan out the door. "Come now, Xan. You have slept half the day away, and there is something magnificent that you absolutely must see."

Games

A crisp wind slapped Xan's cheeks as Brother Andrew led him around the abbey's stone structures—some connected by covered walkways—gesturing and explaining as they walked.

Their first stop had been the abbey church, with its vast empty center and high-arched ceilings that drew the eye to Heaven. Carved statues dotted the little alcoves, and beeswax candles gave off a sweet aroma and glow. A window of many-colored glass rose behind an altar.

"Our priests say Mass here every day in front of this altar," the monk said.

Each building at the abbey had a complicated name and a special purpose. There was the refectory, the large dining room where the monks ate; the dormitory, where they slept; the library, where they studied; the scriptorium, where they hand-copied the Sacred Scriptures; and other places too numerous to recall.

The monk pointed to an eight-sided structure with a sharply pointed roof and a single window. "That is our chapter house. We often meet there to conduct abbey business."

Maybe Hardonbury had special buildings like this, too. He might have worked in one with his father, threshing wheat or cleaning tools or some other task that made calluses on his hands.

They continued along a cobblestone path and came upon a rock house barely large enough for one person. "That," Brother Andrew said, "is our abbot's house. Under *The Rule*, we monks obey his commands as though coming from God. He is as wise and just as he is advanced in age."

The monk reached into a fold in his robe and pulled out a wooden cross. "I almost forgot. Keep this. Our abbot whittled it as a gift for you while you were healing. Use it to pray."

The cross fit neatly in Xan's palm. Unlike the one in the monk's cell, this cross didn't have the figure of Jesus on it. Each of the whittled bumps in the wood felt smooth to the touch.

"How do I use it?" he asked.

The monk raised the brow over his blue eye. "You might not recall, but our Lord Jesus died on a cross for love of us all. When you hold that cross, say your prayers and know you are loved."

Xan passed his thumb along the bumps. The Lord—Creator of all things—dead upon a cross: he somehow knew about that puzzling notion, yet no prayers came to mind. Maybe no one ever had taught him to pray. He stuck the cross safely in his leather pouch.

They left the stone buildings behind them and passed through a gate into a golden field of wheat. Strange that he should know it was wheat, rather than barley or rye.

A throng of workers in brown tunics harvested the wheat while others threshed it in the distance—*thump, thump.* Another man tended sheep in a pasture with a black-and-white dog.

"These men aren't wearing robes, like that man in the refectory," Xan said. "Why not?"

Brother Andrew nodded, as though he approved of the question. "Many come to work here in the granges, especially at harvest time. Some are lay brothers; others are monastery servants."

"Like slaves?"

"Of course not." The monk wavered. "Though I suppose we are all slaves for Christ, each serving in his own way. Monks pray and study; these men make sure our abbey is productive."

Xan peered at his brown tunic and touched a callous on his hand. "Am I to become a servant and work in the granges if we can't find my parents?"

Brother Andrew smiled. "A boy with so many intelligent questions? You can aspire to much more than that. But do not fear, Xan. We shall not rest 'til we find your parents."

Coming to the edge of the granges, they climbed a gently sloping grassy hill. The abbey's structures jutted behind them; a woodland stretched to the left, with a row of hedges and a trail that led under the trees. A green meadow stretched out below, leading to other stone buildings.

In the distance walked two girls dressed in white, carrying bundles of cloth. The taller girl's thick, shimmering hair blew in the breeze, blacker than a monk's robe.

"There are girls at the abbey, too?" Xan said.

"They live in the convent down that lane." Brother Andrew pointed to a broad building at the end of a dirt road that began at the bottom of the hill. "The abbess and her nuns care for them. You will see them from time to time delivering linens and such to our abbey's chamberlain."

There was something captivating about that girl with the black hair. Too bad he wouldn't get a chance to speak with her before tomorrow, when he would return home to Hardonbury.

The monk led him down the hill to a two-story building—the boys' dorm. A solid door with a ringed, metal handle stood open. Inside, at the bottom of a flight of stairs, sat the monk with the untamed gray eyebrows. He held a large scroll in his hands, and his lips mouthed silent words.

Brother Andrew smiled widely. "Leo, I have brought you a visitor. Call him Xan."

The old monk turned a fiery eye on Xan. "Aye, we have already met." He pointed at the door. "The others are coming in from their chores, Andrew. Take him to them. I am praying right now."

Brother Andrew led Xan outside, where laughter had begun to echo from around the side of the dorm. A dozen boys had gathered into two messy groups on the grassy meadow. They wore tunics of brown, white, and black, similar to Xan's. Joshua was there too, standing with a group of younger boys while a few of the older ones barked commands.

Xan straightened his back and gritted his teeth. He must have made friends before, so he should probably trust his instinct to stand tall and strong, even if his throbbing head felt weak.

"Children," Brother Andrew said. "This is Xan."

Joshua waved to him from the edge of one group, a long grin on his freckled face.

"He will be with you for . . . for tonight, at least," the monk said. "Be kind to him; he is still recovering from an injury to his head. Indeed, I am afraid he has lost his memory."

"So he can't remember anything?" Joshua asked, his red hair flopping over his eyes.

"Not a thing," Brother Andrew said.

The monk should have left that detail out. A few boys were snickering about it. One burly-looking boy—broad shoulders, hairy arms, and a permanent smirk on his lips—whispered something to another boy. Maybe they were planning on playing a trick on Xan.

"Well, then." Brother Andrew gave Xan a supportive pat on the back. "Brother Leo will take good care of you tonight. I will see you again tomorrow."

With that, the monk headed back up the hill, maybe to say more prayers. Being with these other boys would probably turn out fine, but Brother Andrew had been kind and had wanted Xan to understand things. Brother Leo and these lads seemed much less interested in his welfare.

As the boys clustered into groups again, Joshua tugged on Xan's tunic. "How old are you?"

An easy question. "I . . . I don't remember." He could count to twenty yet did not know his age. It was as if someone had stuck a firebrand into his memories and seared only certain ones.

Joshua looked him up and down. "Older than me, that's for sure. When were you born?"

Inquisitive little Joshua was likely to ask a hundred "easy" questions he couldn't answer. All his "I don't knows" would become a bore to the boys, and soon they would hate him for it.

Instead of answering, Xan pointed to the others. "What's this you're playing here, Joshua?"

The child burst into a grin. "'Tis called barres." He led Xan to the others. "Can Xan play?"

The burly, hairy boy strutted over. He was Xan's height, with limp, sandy hair and arrogant eyes. "I don't s'pose you know how to play."

Joshua tugged at Xan's tunic again. "That's John. He's captain of the other team."

Xan paused before answering John's question. Surely he must have played games back in Hardonbury. This barres game seemed popular, so why didn't he know the rules?

He shrugged. "I don't think so. I really can't remember."

John shook his head in disgust. "You're going to be quite the nuisance, aren't you? Well, you're not going to be on my team, that's for certain. Morris, you can have him."

A lanky boy stepped over and eyed Xan closely. That must be Morris, the other team captain. He was so tall that Xan's nose barely reached his shoulders.

"You look strong enough," Morris said. "You'll do. Teach him the rules, Joshua."

As the boys formed into two lines—team captains placing them in order—Joshua explained how to play. John's team would send out its first player, who would be chased by the first player from Morris's team. Then John's second player would be sent out to tag Morris's first player, while Morris's second player was sent out to chase John's second player. John's third player would then chase Morris's second, and so on. In this way, each boy had a target to tag while avoiding being tagged themselves. Whichever team tagged all its targets first would win.

"'Tis great fun!" Joshua said.

Except Brother Andrew hadn't let Xan search for his parents today because he needed rest. Running wildly about a meadow couldn't possibly be good for healing. If he hurt himself again, the monk might make him wait even more days to go to Hardonbury. Plus, his head still throbbed.

"Ready, set, and go!" John said, as his first runner took off, sprinting across the field.

"Go!" shouted Morris to his first player, who chased after John's first runner.

Soon both teams scampered about in all directions, laughing and hollering.

Xan's turn was coming up. Should he play? If he didn't play well, the boys would think him stupid *and* slow. That wouldn't matter after tomorrow, but what if he never found his parents?

"You're up, Xan," Morris yelled. "You tag David." He pointed to the tallest boy on John's team, with dark curly hair that desperately needed trimming. "And go!"

David was fast. Within seconds, he'd already caught his target and was running over the grass toward a circle of neatly trimmed bushes with a wide fountain at its center.

"He's getting away, Xan!" Joshua shouted from behind. "Run faster!"

Xan tried to speed up, but his feet refused to cooperate. He might have been a strong runner back in Hardonbury, but the drum crashing in his head was making every step unbearable.

"Tag, I got you!" Hands pushed Xan from behind, causing him to stumble clumsily.

What a disaster—he'd already been tagged. And David, perched on the ledge of the fountain, was hooting out rude animal noises. Maybe Xan should have gone inside to lay down.

He reached the fountain, constructed of smooth, flat rocks of all shapes and sizes. It held a pool of still water—only a couple of feet deep—and several striped, greenish fish swimming beneath.

"Slowpoke!" David sprinted toward the dorm, his dark curls refusing to blow in the wind.

Xan stopped to catch his breath. This was not going well at all. He held his pounding head in his palms and leaned on the ledge as the striped fish meandered in circles. As he looked into the water, his reflection stared back: eyes brown and wide, head as round as a ball, high cheeks, and ears with tips that stuck out from his straight brown hair.

He shouldn't have been here playing dumb games when his parents were out *there* somewhere searching for him. Maybe they were in the woodlands right now, calling his true name.

Just then, a voice did call out, but not from his parents. It was a girl. She sounded panicked.

He looked in the direction of the cry. Several boys had gathered round in a circle on the grass outside the dorm. The girl's shout had come from the center of that circle.

"Oh, no!" Xan pounced off the ledge and sprinted toward the dorm.

5

Lucy

Xan ran while the *boom, boom, boom* crashed in his head.

As he got closer to the dorm, the girl's voice rang out again. "Leave me alone!"

Jeering boys shouted over one another.

"She's afraid of warts!"

"She's gonna cry."

"Don't let her go!"

Joshua ran out to meet him. "You have to help Lucy!"

Why him? He was the newest boy at the abbey; all he wanted was to go home. Is this the kind of thing he'd done back in Hardonbury, running from place to place rescuing girls in distress?

Too out of breath to speak, he kept on until he reached the rim of the circle.

"Lucy, Lucy, smells like a goosey," one of the boys mocked.

Six boys surrounded the black-haired girl—her soft, brown eyes moist with anger. She wore a dainty belt around a white, ankle-length tunic. A speck of a mole graced her pale cheek. She seemed about the same age as Xan.

"I told you to let me pass," Lucy said, her voice strong and crisp.

The other delivery girl must have slipped out of the circle and fled back to the nuns, because she was nowhere in sight.

"What's going on here?" Xan said, barely able to talk as he huffed.

"Well, well, look who's here: our forgetful new friend, Sire Clumsy."

Of course, it was John, the leader of all the mischief. His muscular arm held a huge, croaking toad toward Lucy. She pushed his hand away.

Xan's interruption gave her a chance to escape. She bolted to the edge of the circle, but one of the hooligans grabbed her hair and yanked her back. She cried out in pain.

"Stop this!" Xan said in his sternest voice. But why should John listen to him—a boy with no memory who'd quickly got tagged and bumbled like a fool?

John laughed. "What's the matter? I found this cute toad and wanted to show it to the delivery girl, is all." He stuck the terrified creature in Lucy's face again.

"Let me out of here," she said calmly.

Xan tried to keep his voice as calm as hers. "Let her go." Maybe someone at Hardonbury had taught him it was best to speak with reason when standing up to a bully.

John didn't move.

Just then, the throbbing in Xan's head flashed with light—maybe a memory: a scarred horseman in black, sneering down at a group of men with shovels and hoes. Then it was gone.

A rush of anger pulsed from his head to his hands. If he'd had a stone in his palm he would have thrown it with all his might. The impulse overwhelmed him; his fists shot up in front.

"Oh, really?" John said, dropping the toad. "So you want to fight then."

Lucy turned and ran. David stepped aside as she escaped past him toward the trail that led to the convent.

Xan's head cleared. He stared down at his fists. Why was he so filled with rage? John was a bully, true, but that had nothing to do with him. Except John had picked on an innocent person, and Xan suddenly hated anyone who used power to harm the weak. Maybe he'd seen such injustices at Hardonbury. His parents would know.

Xan dropped his fists to his side.

"That's what I thought," John said. Several boys snickered in the background.

John stepped toward him. "Don't look so grumpy. We weren't gonna hurt her."

Xan shook his head and walked from the circle. "Only cowards pick on girls."

"Is that so?" John said. "Then come teach this coward a lesson."

Xan didn't look back. All that mattered was waking up in the morning healthy enough to walk to Hardonbury with Brother Andrew.

Suddenly Brother Leo stormed out of the dormitory with a paddle. Several boys scurried out of his path, but John stood his ground.

"I saw all that from the window, you rascal," the monk said, grabbing John's arm and paddling at his backside three times hard. "Scripture says to discipline your body and make it your slave! Only with discipline will you be saved, you unruly child."

John fell to the grass, his eyes glistening, his face bright red.

The monk pointed the paddle at the group. "Now, go get washed for the evening meal."

The others scattered around Xan, but Lucy stood on the trail to the convent, her hair dark as night. She was looking this way. Hopefully she'd seen John get punished for what he'd done.

Perhaps he should check to make sure she was all right. He jogged down the path until he reached where she stood. She'd waited for him.

For a moment, all he could do was stare—her eyes were more soft and her face more perfect than anything he'd seen in this new life of his.

She cast her gaze to the ground, and her cheek grew rosy red.

"Are you well?" he asked.

She nodded. "Thank you for helping me. Did that John try to fight you?"

He shrugged. "I'm all right. Brother Leo took the paddle to him, anyway."

"Good. I'm Lucy, by the way." Her smile chased all the pain from his head.

"You can call me Xan. I can walk with you to the convent."

"That would be fine," she said.

They strode side by side in silence as the stone convent drew near.

What could he say to her? Surely he'd never spoken with a girl as pretty as this one in Hardonbury or anywhere else. If he told her about his memory, she might think him dumb.

"I haven't seen you at the abbey ere today," Lucy said.

"I just got here. I . . . I was injured. I'll probably be going home tomorrow."

She stopped walking. "Good for you. I've been here for months with no end in sight."

"Did you lose your parents, too?" Maybe she was just like him.

She shook her head. "Father's left me here 'til his duty is done. He serves the lord of my manor. Last year, the king called our lord to service, and Father had to travel away with him again."

"Your father knows King Henry? That's amazing!"

Lucy smiled. "Don't sound too excited about the king, especially around all these monks here. You know, the king and the Church, they don't get along well at all."

"Nay, I didn't know that." Or if he had known it, he'd forgotten it like everything else.

"Anyway, Father doesn't really know the king. He mainly cares for the noblemen's horses."

"And doesn't your mother miss you when you're gone?" he asked.

"She died when I was a baby." Her eyes narrowed. "She was taking me to see her family in Sicily. That's where Father had met her while traveling abroad. She got sick—a plague."

Lucy had shared so openly with him. She probably wouldn't judge his flaws too harshly.

"I don't remember my parents," he said. "To be honest, I can't remember much of anything since the injury. I'm going to Hardonbury tomorrow to find them."

Just then, a woman stepped out the convent door, garbed in a black robe similar to the ones worn by the monks. A habit covered her head but not her youthful face.

"Lucy," she said, her lips turned down. "You know the rules." Her voice was gentle but reproving. This must be one of the nuns who cared for the girls.

Lucy's cheeks flushed red again. "Sorry, Sister Regina. 'Tis a long story."

What rules had Lucy broken? "Did I get you into trouble?"

She grinned. "We're not permitted to walk alone with boys, but don't worry. Sister Regina will understand when I explain it all to her."

She curtsied politely to him. "'Twas a pleasure to meet you, Xan. I hope you find your family tomorrow."

He waved as Lucy took Sister Regina's hand and entered the convent.

Perhaps it would be all right if he got stuck here at Harwood Abbey a few extra days waiting for his parents. There at least would be one friend for him to get to know better.

"Boy!" An outraged voice echoed from the other end of the path. "Get yourself back here this instant or I will take the paddle to you."

It was Brother Leo. The old monk wasn't joking, either. Even from this distance the heavy paddle in his hand was visible.

Xan jogged back up the trail. If he were lucky, Brother Leo might forgive him for coming down here to check on Lucy instead of washing for the evening meal.

Whatever his punishment might be, though, it will have been worth it.

6

Fear

The dormitory had a sleeping area on the second floor, with low wooden beds lined in rows and stuffed with straw. Brother Andrew had said the dorm used to house novices—boys studying to be monks—prior to the plague that had brought all these other children to the abbey.

Now the novices lived in a corner of the monks' dormitory.

Xan sat on his bed near a narrow window that overlooked the meadow. The others sat on their beds, too. After Brother Leo's paddling of John earlier, the boys seemed ready to obey.

The monk stood in the center of the room with a candle. In the dark of the night, the yellow flame cast shadows from his gruff eyebrows onto his wrinkled forehead.

Xan's eyes grew heavy with weariness. This day had started with him waking in the infirmary and angering Brother Leo, then touring the abbey with Brother Andrew, meeting all the boys and playing a game, then defending Lucy and getting to know her. After that, Brother Leo took them all to a light supper in the refectory before heading back to the dorm for night prayers.

Through it all, his headache had persisted. Only a blessed sleep could take him away from it and heal his body for tomorrow's journey to Hardonbury.

Brother Leo read to them from his thin book—something about God loving everyone, even while they were sinners. Then the monk led the boys in prayer in a foreign tongue he called Latin.

All the while, Xan held the abbot's whittled cross in his palm. It didn't help him remember any prayers, though. God was good, that much he knew. God had rules, too. Most important, God could do anything He wanted, which was a great reason to pray. God could help find his parents or get him back to Hardonbury, or even bring Lucy back up the abbey path.

Brother Leo blew out the candle and finished his prayer in the dark: "Come visit us this night, O Lord, that we may rise at daybreak to rejoice in the resurrection of Christ, your Son, who lives and reigns for ever and ever. Amen."

Then the monk exited the door, speaking as gently as ever. "Sleep in peace, lads."

With the door shut, a single beam of moonlight shone through a crack in the wooden panel that covered the window and kept out the night chill. No one dared speak until the faint footsteps of the monk finally echoed down the stairs. Then some of the boys whispered to each other.

Xan lay still. Tomorrow everything would be different. He might even find his memories, along with his parents. Earlier, there had been a flash of light in his head and a scarred man on a horse. If that had been a memory, it could mean something. Maybe more memories would come.

"Xan." A whisper. "Xan, wake up."

He opened his eyes. Joshua stood over him. How long had he been sleeping?

"What's the matter, Joshua?"

"Come here." He grabbed Xan's hand and pulled him from the straw mattress. The cold wood on his bare feet shot chills through his legs.

Joshua led him to a pair of beds, where John and David sat.

"What's *he* doing here?" John said.

"Tell him," Joshua said. "Tell Xan about the Shadow we saw."

This is what Joshua had been talking about this morning, but it must be a mistake. The angel of death might roam freely in dreams, but not upon the meadow of a holy abbey. Surely God wouldn't allow that.

"Aye, we saw it," John said, turning toward a young boy who had pulled his covers up to his nose. John pointed at the child. "Maybe it comes for *this* one tonight."

The child whimpered, and his fear seemed to feed John's meanness. "A dark robe," he said in a creepy whisper, "gliding over the ground with a blade in its hand—like a ghost, searching for souls to cut away forever."

The child's sniffles grew louder.

Joshua's head nodded up and down. "See, Xan?"

Whether they'd seen a shadow or not, John was using this simply to terrorize the little ones. Why did he have to do that to them? These boys had come to this abbey for protection, not persecution. Xan might be leaving tomorrow, but at least he could help this child now.

"Are you knotty-pated, John?" he said. "Use your head. If this scary shadow is prancing all over the abbey taking people's souls, then why hasn't anyone died yet?"

John flashed a victorious smirk. "Ha! Someone *did* die the night we saw the Shadow. Remember, David?"

David's eyes widened under his dark curls. "Aye. 'Twas the night Father Joseph died."

Xan had no witty comeback to that bit of news. That must be what Joshua was trying to tell him this morning in the refectory, before Brother Andrew had interrupted. Unless this was a prank John and David were playing on him and the other boys.

"Well," Xan said. "I don't know anything about any Father Joseph, but—"

John laughed. "You don't know anything about *anything*."

Xan didn't respond. John wouldn't bait him into a fight. None of it mattered anyhow. Tomorrow he'd be gone. For now, if the children could just see that one of the older boys wasn't afraid, it might bring them some comfort. That might be all he could do in one night.

Xan led Joshua back to bed. "Joshua, don't you worry about all this. 'Tis probably just one of the black monks walking about the grounds. You'll see. There's nothing to fear."

"Oh, believe me," John said, his eyes squinting. "Wait and see—there's plenty to fear."

Xan awoke refreshed. Even his headache had gone, along with the unpleasantness of the night before. In the sweet light of day, no amount of talking about shadows could scare anyone.

Brother Leo escorted the boys to the refectory for a meager breakfast of berries and bread. Then Xan swept the dormitory while the monks completed their morning prayers.

Brother Andrew finally arrived, ready for the first step in their plan.

It was too bad the monk had to spend an entire day going back and forth to Hardonbury on account of him. Surely Brother Andrew would be glad to get back to his prayers once Xan got back to his parents, or whoever might take him in at Hardonbury today—maybe an uncle or cousin.

The monk led Xan along a path that scaled a small hill and plunged into the woodland heading toward Hardonbury Manor. The leaves on the trees were already changing—red, orange, yellow, and brown. From this distance, the tall abbey church stood as a beacon in a sea of color.

"You cannot see it from here," Brother Andrew said, pointing over the distant trees, "but through that forest lie the two villages ruled by our abbey—Penwood Manor and Oakwood Manor. They help sustain Harwood Abbey with food, clothing, and other necessities."

After a brief rest, they journeyed into the woodland, following a slender trail that wound under the shadows of trees. As the trail narrowed, the trunks pressed in on all sides.

For a moment, it sounded as though something had rustled the branches to their left. Maybe it was just his imagination. Brother Andrew didn't seem to notice, talking cheerfully about the history of the abbey and how it had acquired its two prosperous manors.

"The only problem," Brother Andrew said, "is that when an abbey gains too many riches, 'tis difficult to keep an attitude of prayer and sacrifice. Some monks fall away."

A branch cracked, again to the left.

Something must be there. It must be watching Xan, wanting to hurt him. Hunting him, like in his nightmare when his foot had been stuck in that hole. He'd known that creature was coming for him, too.

Still, Brother Andrew was lost in his words: "That is why monks must live apart from the secular world. We must avoid its temptations and greed, supported by our religious community."

If only the monk would stop talking long enough to listen.

"Brother, stop!"

The monk's face widened with surprise. "Is something amiss, Xan?"

"Aye. It feels like—" He scanned the greenery for movement.

At that moment, an animal crashed through the brush and raced toward them with a foul snort. Its short legs held the weight of a massive humped body upon them.

"Boar!" shouted Brother Andrew, pushing Xan out of the way.

The breath rushed from his lungs and he coughed. An anxious pain shot through his chest.

Nay! Now Brother Andrew was in the creature's path.

The boar charged—gray, hairy, and filthy—lowering its two pointed tusks.

"Watch out, Brother!"

As large as a wolf, it gored at the monk's black robe and knocked him to the dirt.

"Up a tree," the monk cried, as the boar circled round for a second charge. "Hurry!"

Xan grasped a low-hanging branch and pulled up his feet. Sharp tusks passed below.

This was like the boar in his dream, except that one had possessed a hideous, malformed snout.

Another light flashed in his mind: a scarred man with a malformed nose holding a sturdy mace. Just as quickly, the memory faded, if that's what it was.

"Boars are unpredictable creatures," Brother Andrew said, striding to a tree and swinging his legs onto a low branch. "Jude's folly, it may be feeding in this area today."

The boar disappeared into the foliage, its din of smashing leaves and branches echoing in the distance. The forest grew quiet.

Brother Andrew slid down and took a thick, dead branch into hand. He stood very still—branch at the ready—awaiting another attack. A long moment passed.

"Come now," the monk said. "We must move away quickly from this area."

Xan jumped down from the branch, and the pair doubled their pace along the path.

The boar must have given up. The sense of danger was lessening with every step.

"Brother?" Xan said, when it was safe. "I . . . I think I may have seen things . . . things that happened. Maybe memories." He described his two flashing visions.

"Excellent. See how God can bring good even from a boar's wrath. Our prior, Father Clement, says your memories may come back slowly at first, but one day the rest will return in a rush, like a thunderstorm. That is how it happened for the monk he knew."

"But what do the visions mean?"

Brother Andrew shut his blue eye but kept the brown one open as he reflected. "Perhaps the man was a . . . Nay, I shall not guess."

"Please, Brother, no more secrets. What else do you know?"

"I cannot—" The monk paused and put a hand to his clean-shaven chin. "Yet there is a place, Xan—a place of danger; one that may spur on more memories. Come, I will show it to you."

7

Homecoming

They walked in silence until they arrived at a winding root that stuck up across the trail, high and round like a serpent's back.

"Ah," Brother Andrew said. "This is the place where danger overtook you that day."

Xan inched toward it. No present danger—just a root. No reason to fear. It wouldn't strike at him like a real serpent; how foolish to even think that. Yet this was the very place that had stolen his life away—his parents, his home, his memory.

"This is where I fell?" he asked. "Who found me here?"

The monk shook his head. "Never mind about that. Just thank our Lord we did find you."

So, there were even more secrets. But what difference did it make who had found him?

He gazed at the root, with the dirt path on all sides of it. Even if he had tripped on the root, how would he have injured his head? That scarred man from his visions had held a mace high, as if to strike. Strike who? Maybe Xan hadn't fallen and banged his head at all.

He put his finger to the sore spot on his skull.

"I was attacked here, wasn't I?" he said. "Struck by the man in my vision."

Brother Andrew didn't answer for a long moment. "That gash on your skull was not caused by simply falling and banging your head, my son. You must have fought him off bravely."

So the monks always had known about the attack. Brother Andrew must believe he'd fought off a fearsome attacker and survived. "That's why you called me Alexander."

The monk nodded. "Well done."

"But why would anyone attack *me*?" He was just a peasant boy, a wheat-thresher.

Brother Andrew shrugged. "Try to remember."

Xan knelt by the root and touched it. He must have tripped over it. Maybe he'd been fleeing a band of forest thieves. Or he might have found a killer's hideout and needed to escape.

Try to remember.

But no more memories came.

The monk moved close and placed a hand on Xan's shoulder. "Come, my son. There will be other chances for you to remember today."

He rose slowly and followed Brother Andrew. Seeing Hardonbury might help his memory.

They spent the next while hiking the woodland trail, but no matter how often he thought about his attacker—the jagged scar, the bent and swollen nose, the horse, the men with shovels, the powerful mace—no other memories would return.

They continued until the sun shone directly above. Brother Andrew abruptly dropped to his knees on the trail. He moved his hand in the sign of a cross—to his forehead, heart, and both shoulders—saying, "In the name of the Father, and of the Son, and of the Holy Ghost. Amen."

The monk motioned for Xan to do the same, but he just stared back.

"'Tis an ancient prayer, Xan. When we make the Sign of the Cross, our words call upon the Blessed Trinity while our hand identifies us with the cross of Christ our savior."

Except they needed to get to Hardonbury to find his parents and his memories.

"Must you teach me to pray right now, Brother?"

The monk pointed to the sky. "'Tis midday, the sixth hour—a time of prayer at the abbey. When a monk is away from home at prayer time, he must pray the psalms on his own. Kneel, my son."

Xan obeyed while the monk pulled out a small leather-bound parchment secured in his belt. With arms raised to Heaven, he recited a psalm. Other words and prayers followed.

Xan's hands fidgeted.

When Brother Andrew finished praying, they stood together.

"Trusting our Creator in prayer will carry us through life's darkest hours," the monk said. "He wants us to seek His help in our lives."

Except he didn't know any of the monks' prayers.

"But what if you don't know the right words to say?"

"Then say whatever is on your mind, my son. Speak as to a dearest friend. God hears."

Of course, God hears. But does He listen? Would He answer?

"Now come, Xan. Hardonbury is not much farther now."

Brother Andrew led Xan a while longer as the trail headed down a gentle slope toward the end of the woodland. They stopped only briefly to eat a bite of bread and cheese.

Eventually a clearing arose between the trees.

"We have arrived at Hardonbury Manor," the monk announced.

It had been only a few days, but it had felt like an eternity. Now the wait was over. If he were from this village, someone would probably recognize him. He would learn his true name.

They exited the woodland next to a pasture filled with lush grass. Sheep grazed peacefully in groups of four or five, but no one tended the animals.

A few yards more and they entered a wide field of wheat, with tall rows of golden stalks stretching down a hill and surrounded by a wooden fence. No one was cutting or threshing the wheat, even though it was ripe for the harvest.

Had he worked in this exact field? If his parents saw him in the distance, would they rush the field and take him in their arms? His heart was sprinting now—faster than that charging boar.

Brother Andrew pointed toward a hill to the north of the field. "Hardonbury Manor is ruled by its lord, who lives right over—" The monk gasped.

On top of the hill lay the remains of a large stone house, charred black by fire, with its roof entirely destroyed. It had a similar style to some of the buildings at Harwood Abbey.

"What is *that*?" Xan asked.

The monk recovered from his surprise. "That is—that *was* the manor house. Someone has brought it to ruins." Brother Andrew's face paled. "Curses and evil days! The parish church has been destroyed too. Who would harm the temple of God?"

A stone church, smaller than the one at the abbey, stood charred and ruined a small distance from the manor house.

"What about my parents? Where would they have lived?" Probably not in a manor house or a church. They'd be the ones working these fields, but no one was here. Where was everyone?

Brother Andrew put his arm around Xan's shoulders and pulled him closer, supporting him with his strength. "Lord have mercy. Prepare yourself, my son. *There* is the village."

At the bottom of the wheat field, a few cottages with thatched straw roofs stood in a row untouched by fire or destruction. Beyond them lay little else but charred wood and debris, as though a great dragon had swept over the village and burned most of the cottages to the ground with fierce streams of fire. The village seemed entirely deserted of human life.

"But—where did—" The black bread loaf Xan had eaten nearly came back up. With so much devastation, his parents must be gone. Or dead. There would be no brothers or cousins or uncles here for him today.

A tear escaped his disbelieving eyes. Then another. Nay—boys weren't supposed to cry, were they? He breathed in and willed the tears away. But why shouldn't boys cry? Everyone cried.

"Be brave, Xan. Keep up hope. Let us go down and find out what has happened."

The monk led him by the arm on a sorrowful march through the golden meadow and past the row of abandoned cottages that had not been destroyed. The full devastation of the village surrounded them, the pungent aroma of smoked wood and smoldering hay still in the air. Only a handful of cottages with thatched roofs had survived the blaze, scattered throughout the charred blackness of Hardonbury like the last leaves of autumn on a dying tree.

What would he do now that Hardonbury was destroyed? No wonder his parents hadn't come for him. They'd probably fled far away, perhaps thinking he'd died in the fire.

"Who goes there?" a man's voice shouted from inside one of the few surviving cottages.

A guard pushed open the cottage door, holding a spear and shield straight out in defense. He wore a chain-mail shirt, a helmet with a strip of iron that protected his nose, and thick black pants.

"We come in peace," Brother Andrew said in greeting. "May the Lord bless you. I am Brother Andrew and this boy is Xan."

"Strangers are not welcome here," the guard replied, pointing the spear toward the monk.

Brother Andrew did not flinch. "This boy is no stranger, friend. He has lost his memory, but we believe he lived in this village with his family. We have come to find them."

The guard pulled back his spear and stared down at his boots, soiled with black mud. "There are none what are left here to find, Brother."

"What happened to this place?" the monk asked.

The guard's face contorted into hatred. "Godless, heartless, ruthless bandits. Filthy swine attacked without a bit'a warning. Burned the lord's manor house, then the rest."

"And why are *you* here?" Brother Andrew said.

"By order of the lord of the manor, I watch over this cursed disaster 'til the clean-up starts."

"Then take us to your lord," the monk ordered.

Maybe there was still hope. Surely the lord of the manor would know who Xan was and where his family had gone. As ruler of the manor, the lord must know all those things.

But the guard was shaking his head. "Nay. The lord will never come back to his . . . his manor house." He pointed toward the ruins on the hill.

"And what of the priest from the parish church?"

"He left with the manor lord. Both have abandoned this cursed place, never to return. Them what did survive this disaster will serve a new lord when they come back."

Xan's legs wobbled. Brother Andrew held his arm and squeezed it supportively. "Have faith," the monk whispered.

But what faith could remain? His village was destroyed. The manor lord and all his people had fled. Even the priest. His parents might never return, even if they could.

"And what of the survivors?" the monk asked. "Where have they gone?"

"Them what survived fled to their new lord at Chadwick Manor," the guard said.

The monk grinned. "Lord Godfrey!" He turned to Xan. "This is good news, my son. Lord Godfrey rules over Chadwick Manor. Actually, he is lord over many landed estates, but Chadwick is the nearest. It borders the woodland north of Harwood Abbey."

Xan lifted his face from the desolation and studied the monk's eyes. Like a smoking ember in a suffocated fire, there was still hope in them. It seemed to glimmer in his blue eye especially.

Maybe his parents were survivors. Perhaps they'd fled to Chadwick with the others. That would explain why they hadn't come for him. They might even think Xan was dead because he'd disappeared. If he could find them, imagine their joy at discovering their lost son had survived!

"Aye," the guard said. "Them what survived will be back after Lord Godfrey's men show up to clear away all this muck. Them crops still need a harvest, you see."

The guard pointed to the golden fields, which hadn't been touched by the disaster. How odd that almost the entire village should be burned down but the fields spared. Why would the bandits do that? At least those crops would be available to benefit Lord Godfrey, the new lord. Maybe he would share them with the survivors of Hardonbury who had fled there.

"May God go with you," Brother Andrew said, raising a hand to bless the guard.

Nay, they couldn't be leaving already. There could be clues in this debris to spark more memories or even confirm that Xan's family had survived.

"Wait, Brother." Xan turned and addressed the guard. "Please, is there anything left to help me learn something about my family? About who I am?"

The guard refused to meet his eyes. "There is a place, but—" He stopped.

"But what?" Xan said. "Can you take us there?"

The guard looked to Brother Andrew. "It could be hard on the lad."

Brother Andrew nodded, as though he understood. "Be at peace. You may take us there."

The guard led them slowly toward a hill near the south meadow. The way the guard walked, and the way the monk moved his lips silently in prayer, they must be taking him to a burial ground.

As they approached the hill, three rows of wooden crosses rose up on small mounds of dark earth—burial plots. Someone had carved a name into each brown cross.

"There they lie, the bodies of the slain," the guard muttered. "Lord grant 'em peace."

The guard left them alone in the dead quiet; not even a hint of breeze rustled a falling leaf.

Brother Andrew approached the crosses and whispered a prayer for the departed. "May perpetual light shine upon them," he concluded, making the Sign of the Cross.

This could be the moment that would end all moments. Did some of those crosses belong to his family? Would he even know it if he could read the names written on them?

The monk took Xan's hand. "You cannot read these, can you?"

Xan shook his head. This probably wasn't a memory problem, though. Somehow, he knew he had never been taught to read.

"If you wish it, I will teach you to read one day. For now, do not be afraid. I will read to you the blessed names on these crosses. Try your memory again."

Maybe this was the time to pray. If God wanted, He could make Xan remember. He reached in his leather pouch and took out the cross the abbot had whittled. *Help me remember, God.*

Xan knelt as the monk read each name aloud—a total of thirteen. After each name, he closed his eyes tight and concentrated. He could do this. *Please, God. Help me remember.*

The more he tried to force the memories, the more he seemed to scare them away. He threw his arms up. "I can't! I tried to pray, Brother, but it didn't work."

The monk placed a hand on his shoulder. "Do not think you prayed in vain, Xan—God reveals the truth to us in His own time and for our own good. Trust in His holy purposes."

Why bother praying if God was going to do what He wanted anyhow? Or was that the point: that by waiting for the answer to a prayer, a person learned to trust God more?

Xan stood. "I know what we must do, Brother."

The ember of hope from the monk's blue eye seemed to have taken hold in Xan's heart.

"We should go to Chadwick Manor," Xan said. "We must go see this Lord Godfrey."

8

Death

The next morning was Sunday—Brother Andrew had called it the Lord's Day—a day of rest. That meant no chores for the boys, no harvesting for the servants, and no journey to Chadwick. The abbot had approved their plan when they'd returned from Hardonbury last night, but he forbade them to travel until Monday.

Though it was the Lord's Day, Brother Leo still had screamed at two of the younger boys who hadn't made their beds properly. Then he'd escorted all the boys to Mass at the marvelous abbey church with the high-arched ceilings.

Everyone was there: the monks and the novice boys, the nuns and the girls. And Lucy.

Maybe God was answering one of Xan's prayers already. He'd wanted to see her again.

Standing with Joshua in the wide-open center of the church—there were no chairs or benches—Xan listened to the monks' chanting. Candles of beeswax shimmered near the stained-glass window. In an alcove, a statue on a pedestal drew him in: a woman holding a young child in her arms. That must be baby Jesus with His mother, Mary. Her eyes seemed so lifelike. The infant in her arms held out his hands in a sign of peace.

A few monks stood near the altar. Those must be the priests Brother Andrew had told him about yesterday. Priests could do special jobs the other monks could not, such as saying Mass.

A short monk stood and read from an enormous book filled with beautifully drawn squiggly letters and colorful pictures. Then the chanting continued, followed by Sacred Scripture readings.

Surely the boys couldn't understand the words chanted in *Latin*—the strange tongue of the Holy Roman Empire. According to Brother Andrew, the Church's prayers and rituals had been passed down in Latin from century to century because of that empire.

The prior stood to speak. He preached a long time, calling Jesus the "Resurrection and the Life" and explaining that one day every Christian would pass through death into eternal life. "We are all mortal and destined to die," he said. "But death is not the end. Remember the example of our dearly departed friend, Father Joseph. May we all face our deaths with his faith and trust."

A boy coughed down the row—John, smirking and gloating as though the prior had just proved the Shadow had come for Father Joseph's soul the same night John and David had seen it.

Still, could it be possible the stories were true about the angel of death walking the earth in the night, claiming the souls of those destined to die? Like those thirteen poor souls at Hardonbury. Even if the stories *were* true, that didn't mean John and David had truly seen the angel.

When the final chant had ended and everyone started streaming through the soaring doors, Xan dropped back from Joshua and allowed people to pass on both sides. Soon Sister Regina and the other nuns passed, followed by the girls from the convent.

How would he start the conversation with Lucy when it was her turn to pass? She might go by him without even a greeting, as all the others had. Perhaps he should trip over his feet in front of her to get her attention. Nay—then she'd think he really *was* Sire Clumsy.

"Good morrow, Xan." Her soft, sweet voice spoke at his left shoulder.

"Oh! Lucy." He moved to the side. "Good morrow."

"My goodness, where did all the other boys go?" she said. Her lips turned up. She was teasing him, knowing he'd fallen behind to see her. But there was no harm in making a friend with someone who was kind and gentle.

He shrugged and grinned. "They've gone to play barres or something, I guess."

"I didn't expect to see you again," she said. "I thought you were going home."

"Oh, that." As they walked, he told her about his journey to Hardonbury.

As his story grew more sorrowful, her playful eyes retreated. "I'll pray for you and your family today," she said. "I can't imagine how horrid all this must be for you."

She seemed to understand it all so naturally. He hadn't needed to explain how he felt.

"Brother Andrew and I are going to see this Lord Godfrey tomorrow."

Lucy's face lit up in surprise. "Godfrey, the rich land baron? Do you think he'll see you?"

Lord Godfrey must have been very great indeed for Lucy to know about him, although her father apparently tended horses for all sorts of powerful men.

"Well, he is the new lord of Hardonbury," Xan said. "I imagine he'd be willing to meet with one of his own people."

Lucy shook her head. "You really don't understand all this, do you?"

Warmth filled his cheeks as he bowed his head in shame.

Lucy seemed startled. "Nay, I didn't mean to sound like that! The only reason I know any of this is because Father travels with these barons and noblemen to London and Lincoln and York."

"Right," he said. "Of course. Then you don't think Lord Godfrey will want to see me?"

"Most manor lords are so busy with their wealthy friends that they don't have time for the simple folk. We are just peasants, after all. And they're like . . . well . . ."

"Like kings," he said.

"Aye. The manor lord is a ruler, and the peasants work the land for him as tenants."

"So we're not important."

She frowned. "Everyone's important, Xan. We're just not important to *them*."

The door to the convent rose before them. They'd walked the entire way together, barely noticing the other girls in front and behind.

Lucy gave a wave. "If you do see Lord Godfrey, be sure to bow when you speak."

"All right. I will."

Lucy slipped through the convent door, her high, black curls vanishing into the crack.

Xan sat at a wooden table in a cottage with two others. A man was eating a loaf of bread with his work-worn hands. A woman—a bit younger-looking than the man, with a warm beauty—was humming a tune that could bring peace to a troubled soul. Xan somehow knew every note of it.

A tap came at the cottage door.

A sickening chill convulsed Xan's body. "Don't open it!" he yelled.

The woman didn't hear him. She moved to the door, as if drawn by the visitor.

"Stop!" he shouted again, louder.

She pressed the handle; the door creaked. A bony hand reached in, along with a black robe.

Except the woman didn't scream or cry or panic. She merely stepped aside and allowed the thing to enter freely, not a bit of fear on her face. She seemed to welcome the shadowy figure.

"Nay!"

Xan woke up, shivering on his straw mattress. Had he screamed aloud or only in his nightmare? And why had the woman let the angel of death into her home so willingly?

He peered about the dormitory. A half-moon shone through his window slit.

In front of the other window stood John, David, and Joshua.

Oh, no. This would be another chance for John to frighten the youngest boys.

He joined the others at the window.

"Xan!" Joshua said. "John just saw the Shadow again!"

"Right now? In the meadow?" He stepped closer to John.

This was it: the time for proof of this supposed shadow. If John was making it all up, Xan could reveal the bully's trick in one defining moment and put an end to the fraud once and for all.

"There—see it?" John was pointing to a clump of trees next to a field, near the hedges and the trail that led to Lord Godfrey's estate. "'Tis moving by the hedge."

Some of the children had awakened now, sitting up in their beds with fearful eyes.

Xan nudged David aside from the window. "Let me get a better look."

"Watch in the trees by the old path." John spoke without arrogance for once.

In all that darkness, John couldn't possibly see much. The moon barely lit the edge of the woodland. A jagged line might have been the tops of hedges, but who could say from this distance?

"I don't see anything, John. 'Tis your imagination. There's nothing—"

At that moment, the line of hedges seemed to tremble as something passed in front of them. It wasn't so much that a shadow could be seen, but rather that the hedges could *not* be seen.

"You see it, don't you?" said John, arrogant once more. "I told you."

As Xan's eyes adjusted to the lighting, the contours of a robe of dark material took form. Aye—a robed figure with a hood covering its head. Something had glistened in its hand, too.

The angel of death was rumored to carry a scythe blade. But in the stories, the only people who could see the angel were those destined to die.

"What *is* that thing?" Xan whispered to himself.

His comment caused two children to cry out, faces muffled in their mattresses. Instead of helping matters, he'd made it all worse. He should have just stayed in bed. Now he needed to do something before the entire dorm was terrified to tears.

"Nay." He stepped back from the window. "A black robe—probably one of the monks."

"Well," said John, his tone cruel and taunting. "Then why don't you go down and speak with him? I'm sure you would have a very nice conversation."

Xan didn't answer.

John was right, of course. Xan could end this right now by going down there. But what if he was right and this were merely a monk? He'd probably get into big trouble. Brother Leo would definitely hit him with the paddle. And maybe the abbot wouldn't let him go to Chadwick Manor tomorrow, either. That was reason enough not to go down.

But was that the real reason? His heart was beating fast; his hands were shaking. Some part of him must be worried the Shadow might be something else. He could make a fatal mistake going down there. And he'd just dreamed of the angel of death in that woman's cottage. Was that a sign?

"Gone!" shouted David, who had taken Xan's spot at the window. "Behind the hedge."

There lay the path toward Chadwick. Now the boys would say the Shadow was going to Lord Godfrey's estate to claim someone's soul.

John let out a mocking laugh. "Well, now we know you're both clumsy *and* a coward."

"I don't care what you say, John. Stay up all night if you want. I'm going back to bed."

Xan marched to his mattress and pulled up the blanket.

If he were lucky, his brave face would at least set some of the younger ones at ease. If they saw him going back to bed, they might feel safe enough to do so too. John was wrong—he had to be wrong. Sometimes stories might be true, but sometimes stories were just stories.

Yet, if John were right, then the Shadow lurked somewhere out there tonight. And someone would have his soul claimed at the very hands of Death.

The morning would reveal the truth.

Godfrey

Brother Andrew and Xan headed toward the hedges and the trail that led to Chadwick Manor. They would be walking in the footsteps of the Shadow this morning.

"Maybe you'll find a dead body on the way there," Joshua had suggested at breakfast.

Nay, the only thing worth finding today was his family. With the sun sparkling above them, all their fear about the Shadow seemed silly. Joshua had even taken a head count in the dorm to make sure none of the others had disappeared in the night.

When they reached the hedges, two novice boys in white tunics passed by. The monk gave a slight wave but said nothing to them.

"If you see any novices, Xan, leave them be. They are in a time of silent prayer this week."

What a strange life for those boys, whose parents had brought them to the abbey and offered them up as novices. Brother Andrew spoke freely about them as he led Xan along the trail to Chadwick, leaves on the path crunching under their leather shoes.

"One day," the monk said, "those novices will take the three vows of the black monks: Conversion—promising to turn from sin and follow God; Obedience—promising to obey *The Rule* and our abbot; and Stability—promising to live at the abbey all their days, except when the abbot sends them off on official business."

But why would any boy want to live like a prisoner at an abbey, far away from his family?

They stopped after an hour for a break before continuing into a part of the woodland where the light grew dim because so many trees clamored for the sun. Brother Andrew seemed to relish the walk, mouthing prayers under his breath a while before sharing another lesson or idea.

"Xan, this morning after *prime*—that is our prayer at dawn—the abbot brought me news from our abbey's two manors, Penwood and Oakwood. It seems no refugees from Hardonbury fled to either place. 'Tis no surprise, though. Chadwick is the closest manor to your village."

The monk's news was good. It meant his family was probably with Lord Godfrey, not spread around at all different manors. If he found them, he would probably stay with them tonight.

In fact, this might be his final time ever to walk with Brother Andrew. The monk hadn't seemed burdened by keeping his company these past days. Maybe he was glad for the chance to leave the abbey for a time because his vow of stability had kept him stuck there for years.

Perhaps Xan's mother and father would let him visit the abbey sometimes to see Brother Andrew and Joshua. And Lucy. Unless his parents were very strict. They'd make him change his name, of course. How odd that would be, going back to Harwood Abbey with a different name.

"Xan is not my true name," he said to the monk at their next resting place. "I hope you won't mind if I start using my old name again."

"Do not worry about that," the monk said, leaning against a tree. "We black monks know quite well that names change. Indeed, my parents did not name me Andrew. That is the name I chose when I took my final vows and entered my new life with God."

That seemed odd, to one day decide to pick a new name. "So, what is your real name?"

"I was baptized Robert, but that name died when I took my vows. Still, whether Robert or Andrew, God loves me just the same, for He sees and loves what is on the inside."

Their journey to Chadwick continued for a long while more, until the trail curved and headed out of the forest. Brother Andrew stopped them at noon to chant his midday prayers, which he called *sext*. They then continued on the path as it led toward Lord Godfrey's estate.

From the crest of a hill, Chadwick Manor came into sight. It seemed much larger than Hardonbury, though arranged in similar fashion. Cottages dotted the center of the village. On every side lay fields and pastures. A stone parish church stood alone, and at the northern end of the estate, a manor house towered to the sky, encircled by a wall. Thin chimneys puffed out wisps of smoke.

"This is the largest of Lord Godfrey's manors," Brother Andrew said.

"How many manors does he have?"

"Too many," the monk said with a laugh. "In each he has appointed a knight to rule the manor in his stead, in exchange for their service and loyalty. And also a share of their profits."

They followed the trail into a wide pasture, where servants tended sheep and goats. A jagged stone wall surrounded the entire manor: too low to stop bandits from entering but probably tall enough to slow them down until Lord Godfrey's guards could arrive to fight.

"Of course, Xan, the lord of all these lands is King Henry—though God is the real Lord, truth be told. When the King needs soldiers in time of war, a land baron like Lord Godfrey must order his knights to fight for the king. 'Tis a tax on him for ruling land in Henry's kingdom."

That sent the monk into another lesson as they followed the path past busy cottages, where peasant women and children swept and did their chores.

For well over a hundred years, the arrangement between king, lord, and tenant had given the King an army ready for battle whenever England was threatened. It had helped the land barons become wealthy, while avoiding the dangers of combat. It had allowed knights to gain wealth, while only occasionally fighting in battle. And it had given peasants—like Xan's family—a place to work and live. It was just as Lucy had said.

But where did Xan fit in? Was his destiny to work with his family for Lord Godfrey, sweeping and harvesting wheat in a run-down little cottage?

They finally arrived at the outer gate to Lord Godfrey's manor house. The thick stone wall rose three times higher than the jagged one around the rest of Chadwick. Upon it stood guards in chain mail, with bows and swords. They signaled the monk, who revealed the reason for their visit.

"Wait there," one of the guards shouted.

Brother Andrew plopped down on a large stone. "Rest yourself, Xan. This could take a while."

"What is Lord Godfrey like?" Xan asked, dropping into a soft patch of yellowing grass.

"He is much like any rich nobleman—busy and proud. He has been a benefactor to Harwood Abbey over the years. He donated that stained-glass window in our abbey church."

"Have you ever spoken with him?"

"Only once. We monks avoid contact with the secular world, especially since King Henry and our Pope have battled so fiercely against each other. The King seeks to rule the Church as he rules his own lands, I think. In any event, Godfrey travels often and is likely to be away today."

Lucy was right about the monks not liking the King. But still, how nice it would be to have wealth like King Henry. Then Xan and his family could live wherever they wanted.

"What does Lord Godfrey do with all his treasure?" he asked.

Brother Andrew chuckled. "By grace, one can only imagine. It costs a great fortune to run his vast lands. And I know too well that those with wealth always seek more. 'Tis never enough."

The gleam in the monk's blue eye hinted that some story might be behind his comment, but before Xan could ask, the gate clanged open.

A tall man in a metal helmet raised a hand in greeting. "Follow me."

He escorted Xan and Brother Andrew to the manor house entrance, explaining that Lord Godfrey was at the manor today and had extended full hospitality to his unexpected visitors. He'd even sent along a welcoming message and invitation to meet with him in person.

"How unusual," the monk said, though clearly pleased by the honor.

They entered through enormous wooden doors graced with a carved inset of two swords that came together over a serpent and a cross. Inside, smooth stone walls shimmered in the torchlight as they passed through wide hallways. At length, they arrived in a lavish reception area with walls decked in ornaments of gold and silver, and tables filled with fruits, nuts, and breads.

A servant approached and bowed. "Might I offer you some refreshment to quench your hunger and thirst after such a long journey?"

Brother Andrew shook his head. "Not a morsel for me. Food at this time of day is strictly forbidden by *The Rule*." He gestured to Xan. "You may have a small helping if you wish."

Xan approached the table and chose a wafer from a silver tray. It unexpectedly melted into pure honey-syrup in his mouth—nothing like the simple meals he'd eaten at Harwood Abbey.

The servant then led them through four impressive halls, each with magnificent tapestries that hung from high ceilings, stretching halfway to the floor. By the time they entered the royal meeting room, Xan's heart was pounding.

Lord Godfrey sat upon a richly adorned chair, wearing a collared, puffy shirt with red, gold, and blue colors sewn throughout its shiny fabric. When he stood, he towered over Brother Andrew by at least a foot. His enormous forehead glistened in the candlelight, distracting from his closely cropped beard and sea-blue eyes that shone with wisdom.

"My good brother," the lord said with a smile. "'Tis a pleasure to see you again. It has been far too long since you last visited."

Brother Andrew returned the greeting with a blessing and a bow. "I am honored that you remember me, my lord. I wish I could enjoy your company more often, but you know our strict routine at the abbey."

"I know it well," Lord Godfrey said.

Any moment now, Brother Andrew would introduce him. Lucy had said to be sure to bow. The monk had bowed so smoothly, as though he weren't at all intimidated by this land baron. Had the monk spent time in his life with important men such as this?

"And this, sire," Brother Andrew said, pointing, "is Alexander."

Lord Godfrey nodded at him without saying a word.

Xan tried to bow, going down almost halfway as the monk had done. "Sire."

After Brother Andrew and the manor lord exchanged further routine pleasantries and local news, Godfrey invited them to sit on a comfortable sofa.

"Unfortunately," Brother Andrew said, "the dark events at Hardonbury Manor have forced me to leave the seclusion of my abbey and seek your assistance."

Godfrey's face drew up in concern. "I hope no evil has befallen your monastery. Or Penwood Manor." The way he'd emphasized the words "Penwood Manor" seemed odd, as though he were more interested in that manor than in the condition of the abbey.

"Nay, my lord."

"Very good," Godfrey said with relief. "I often wish I had the resources to spare some guards to protect your abbey. Indeed, my bailiff has been looking into why our finances have been so stretched lately, despite all our prosperous manors. In any event, my defenses are thin. Only last night, I lost the captain of my guard. A bad heart they say; still, his death was unexpected."

Xan's face suddenly grew cold. A dead guard at Chadwick last night—John would revel in that news. He would claim it confirmed all his theories about the Shadow, just as with Father Joseph's death. This could be a coincidence, of course. But was it possible the Shadow really *did* visit Lord Godfrey's estate last night when it walked upon the trail to Chadwick?

Godfrey continued, "I simply do not have enough men to defend areas outside my estate in these cursed days. If the abbey would return Penwood to my estate, I could then devote resources to protect it. Otherwise, I fear for the safety of your abbey and our dear Penwood Manor."

The monk folded his hands. "As the abbot says: 'We have God to protect us.'"

Lord Godfrey suddenly became tense. "As you know, my dear brother, I have a deep interest in Penwood." His voice grew cold. "If anything were to happen to it. . . . Nay, I pray only that your good abbot would agree that Penwood sits on land I inherited from my uncle."

Brother Andrew kept a pleasant tone. "Come, lord, let us not raise this ancient land dispute. You are always in our prayers, as one of our abbey's most generous benefactors, but on this matter the abbot is unyielding. He will never allow Penwood to join a secular estate like yours."

For a long moment, a cloud lingered over their conversation. If Lord Godfrey got angry, he might not help them find Xan's family. Then this long journey might have been for naught, all because of some disagreement over one of the abbey's manors that had nothing to do with Xan.

The monk's voice grew softer and he pointed at Xan again. "Let me tell you what has brought me out of seclusion this day, my lord. This boy, Alexander, is in need of help."

The brow on the nobleman's vast forehead wrinkled in concern. He put a hand to his graying beard. "How so?" His voice sounded gentler.

Brother Andrew explained Xan's situation.

Godfrey stood, his sea-blue eyes shining. "Alas, poor child! How can I help?"

"Please, sire," Xan said. "Can you find my family? Might they have come here?"

The nobleman nodded. "Some poor villagers fled here from Hardonbury over a week ago."

"Are they still here?" Xan said. His heart thumped so heavily in his ears now that he might not even hear Lord Godfrey's answer. With one wrong word, the nobleman could crush him.

Yet Godfrey said no word. He rang a golden bell that had been on the arm of his chair.

Almost instantly, a mustached man appeared in the doorway, dressed in a thick red shirt of wool, with pants as white as a sheep's coat. His slick brown hair curled at its edges, and his eyes were narrow, as though he were perpetually squinting.

"Aye, my lord?" the man said, bowing. His voice was full and booming.

"This is my bailiff, Sire Roger—one of my finest knights," Godfrey said to the monk.

"Blessings on you," Brother Andrew said with a bow.

"And to you," Sire Roger said. He eyed Xan without saying a word to him.

Godfrey quickly explained why his visitors had come. "I need you to escort the monk and this poor boy to the villagers of Hardonbury. Give them whatever assistance they require."

"It shall be done, my lord," Roger said. He twirled his oily mustache and bowed.

This was it, then. Lord Godfrey would help. Just moments from now, Xan might be in the warm embrace of his mother, explaining to his father where he'd been all these days. Maybe they would know why the scarred man with the bent nose had attacked him in the woodland.

Brother Andrew and the nobleman were already exchanging farewells.

"And send my regards and well-wishes to your good abbot," Godfrey said.

Then he stepped over to Xan. He was so tall, he nearly needed to bow just to place a hand on Xan's shoulder. "Do not worry, boy. You are in good hands with Sire Roger. He practically runs this estate for me. If your parents are here, he will find them for you."

He tousled Xan's hair and smiled.

"Thank you, my lord," Xan said, bowing low. "I shall be forever thankful to you."

"Now, follow me," Sire Roger said, his narrow eyes widening to further reveal their gray coloring. "Let us go find your family."

10

Identity

S ire Roger led Xan and Brother Andrew down a winding staircase and through the Great Hall, as the bailiff called it. The huge room was decorated with glimmering golden plates and silver shields.

On the farthest wall hung the largest tapestry Xan had seen yet. It had the same symbols as those carved in the massive manor doors: two swords coming together over a serpent and a cross. But what did the symbols stand for?

The bailiff noticed his curiosity. "That is the Godfrey seal. Magnificent, is it not?"

"Aye, but what does it mean?" Xan asked.

Sire Roger's eyes grew round. "My father and Lord Godfrey's father heeded the call of Saint Bernard and took up the cross in the last Crusade, liberating Spain from the Moors."

Brother Andrew immediately took an interest. "They sacrificed much for that war. But I hear tell 'tis only a matter of time ere Jerusalem falls again. A new Crusade may come soon."

This might explain why the abbey had that painting of a man with a sword and a cross in his belt, joyfully going off to war. He might have been one of those crusaders.

"But what does this have to do with these symbols?" Xan said.

Sire Roger pointed to the tapestry. "Lord Godfrey's father commissioned this design upon his return from Spain. The serpent is the symbol of the devil, and the cross is the sign of goodness."

In the picture, the evil serpent's fiery red skull seemed to be cracking under the power of the cross. Both swords were aimed squarely at the serpent's head.

"The Godfrey way is to crush the forces of evil with might in the name of God," the bailiff said. "You will find these symbols on the door of our manor and even on my lord's wax seal."

Perhaps Lord Godfrey would let Xan bring his family back to this place to see all these amazing items. His parents had probably lived in a beat-up cottage their entire lives.

"Come now," Sire Roger said, taking them from the room.

They exited the back gate of the manor house and onto a cobbled path that led to the center of the village. While they walked, the bailiff spoke of the estate and all its happenings.

Peasants along the way stopped to greet Sire Roger out of respect. Brother Andrew had said that the larger a nobleman's estate grew, the more important (and wealthy) its bailiff would become. Judging from all the bows and greetings, Sire Roger must be an important man.

They walked through the village, past the horse stables, and out another gate. They arrived at a broad yellow meadow filled with shabby brown tents thrown together in haste. Dozens of ragged men, women, and children filled the meadow, cleaning or talking or simply sitting together.

Sire Roger waved his hand at the tents. "Here we are: the sanctuary area. These poor people are here only a short while. They will return home when the damage is cleared. We can be grateful that

Hardonbury's fields survived the attack unscathed and will bring in a rich harvest for us."

"'Tis very Christian of Lord Godfrey to help them," Brother Andrew said.

"Aye. He has a trusting heart."

Xan just stared. He might be looking at his parents right now and not even know it. Would they be angry that he'd been gone all this time, or would they scoop him up in their arms in relief? Yet no one in the meadow was turned toward him. If one of them would just look, they might recognize him and lead him to his family.

"I do not know any of these peasants," Sire Roger said. "But let us start with that one."

He pointed to a woman standing near a tent. Her long, clinging tunic was filthy and torn. As they approached, her odor grew so foul that Xan had to pinch his nose.

"Be charitable, my son," Brother Andrew said, frowning at Xan's reaction.

Xan dropped his hand back to his side. Yet the bailiff kept his own hand near his mouth.

Unlike the peasants of Chadwick, these villagers had not gone out of their way to greet Sire Roger as they passed. Still, when they reached the woman, she gave a slight curtsy to them.

Sire Roger nodded but kept his hand over his mouth and nose.

"The Lord be with you, good woman," Brother Andrew said with a smile.

"And with you," she said. The lines of sorrow on her brow smoothed a bit at his blessing.

"I am Lord Godfrey's bailiff," Sire Roger said. "We require your assistance."

"Oh, really? *My* help?" As she spoke, she glimpsed Xan. Her eyes lit up in recognition.

"I am Brother Andrew of Harwood Abbey," the monk said. "Do you know this child?"

She nodded. "I seen him in Hardonbury—" she glanced at the rows of tents all around her—"ere we come to all this."

It was all true then. He really was a boy from Hardonbury, just as the monks had said. He was closer than ever to finding his family now.

"Do you know my parents?" Xan blurted, stepping closer to the woman. "My real name?"

She cast her gaze downward. "These days, I can barely keep my own kin's names in this old mind. But I know you used to run the East Meadow with the other lads."

Xan clenched and squeezed at his hands. "And my family?"

The woman paused.

"Answer us, woman," Sire Roger said. "Do you know his family or not?"

She shrugged. "He had a mother and father, but where they are, I couldn't say. The village was all ablaze when I legged it outta there."

"Please," Xan said. "Can't you tell me anything about who I am?"

A tear streamed from her eye. She gestured toward a man standing near another worn tent. "Ask Old Tom. He knows everyone's business."

In a charred brown tunic, Old Tom seemed even filthier than the old woman. It must have been more than Sire Roger could bear.

"I begin to feel ill," the bailiff said. The foul grimace on his face and spittle on his mustache left no doubt about the revulsion he felt. "I pray I must take my leave of you. But if there is anything you require—anything at all—ask the guards on the perimeter there to fetch me."

"Thank you, sire." The monk gave the customary bow. "May God reward your kindness."

As the bailiff jogged off, Brother Andrew led Xan to Old Tom. The monk offered a blessing and explained their situation to the man, who ran his fingers through his coarse, jagged beard.

A few of the other villagers a distance away were pointing toward Xan—two boys and a woman. Could that be his mother and brothers? Surely they'd be running to him.

Old Tom's bushy eyebrows came together as he peered at Xan. "'Course I remember the lad," he said. "That be Helen and Nicholas's boy."

"Then you know who I am?" Xan exclaimed. "You know my family?"

Old Tom nodded but directed his gaze to the monk. "The lad got no brothers or sisters."

"And his name?" the brother pressed.

"Name?" Old Tom said. "'Tis Stephen, of course. I wondered what happened to you, Stephen. Just disappeared, you did."

"Stephen," Xan said in a whisper. Nothing. No memory. No familiarity.

If Tom knew this much about him, why wasn't he pointing out his parents? Did they not flee to Hardonbury with the others? They should be shouting "*Stephen!*" from across the meadow.

"And what about my mother and father?" he pressed.

Old Tom scratched at his beard but said nothing.

"Do you know the fate of the boy's parents?" Brother Andrew asked, more gently.

Old Tom's face dropped. "Well now . . ." He stumbled over some muttered words.

"Please. What happened to my parents?"

Old Tom's hesitation could mean only one thing, yet Xan's heart couldn't possibly give up yet. Not now. Not here.

Tom finally said, "Must I speak it, Brother? How do you tell a lad his mother and father aren't comin' home no more? We're all cursed, I say. Those bandits . . ." A tear rolled down the man's wrinkled cheek as his words faded into silence.

In the rows of crosses on the hill at Hardonbury Manor, had Brother Andrew read out the names Nicholas and Helen? Had he stood near the graves of his parents while the monk prayed?

The wound on his head from the scarred man pulsed. He felt dizzy. The honey-sweet wafer he'd eaten rushed its way to the top of his throat, out his mouth, and onto the grass.

Brother Andrew looped an arm around his waist to provide support. "Easy, my son. Come and sit down."

He fell into the grass and let his head rest upon the cool green blades while Old Tom spoke with the monk in a hush. Whatever else the man would say couldn't possibly matter.

All this time, there'd been no one looking for him. They were all gone. He was even worse off than those novice boys whose parents had dropped them off at the abbey. At least their families could visit once a year. They could go home if they wanted. Where could *he* go now?

He had a name—Stephen—but no family, no memories to go with that name.

He was alone in the world.

They journeyed in silence for most of the way back to the abbey. He walked a step behind Brother Andrew, palming the cross he'd taken from the leather pouch on his waist. The monk held beads in his hand and murmured prayers that he said would bring peace to the souls of the dead.

Brother Andrew's words brought little comfort. No prayers would change the fact he would never have parents to embrace him, never have a joyful reunion with brothers and sisters.

When they were close to the abbey, they rested at a crossing of trails that stretched out in four directions—one trail led to Harwood Abbey, while the others led to Penwood Manor, Oakwood Manor, and Lord Godfrey's estate. Brother Andrew leaned against a marking stone.

"What happens next, Brother?" With no family to claim him, he was no different than any other orphan at the abbey now. "Must I stay in that dorm forever?"

Bullying from John; protecting the young boys; worrying about the Shadow—was this to be his life now? Not to mention paddles and yelling from Brother Leo.

"Where else would you go, my son?" the monk asked.

After today, there *wasn't* anywhere else to go. "Nowhere."

"As far as what happens next," the monk said, "that depends on the Lord. The Living God is not a character in a story book, Xan. If you are open to hearing His voice, He just might speak to you—in your prayers, in your conversations, even in your dreams."

In my dreams.

Last night he'd dreamt of the woman who'd let the angel of death freely into her cottage. Could that have been God trying to warn him that his mother had already died?

"I did have a strange dream last night," he said.

He described it for the monk, who seemed to take his story seriously.

"Do you think God was speaking to me?"

Brother Andrew nodded. "It might be so. Ere Jesus was born, Saint Joseph received God's Word in his dreams. The three kings from the East also received a message from the Lord in their dreams after they visited the child Jesus, as did many saints and apostles. Yet we must be careful to discern the meaning of our dreams by seeking wise counsel. And through prayer."

They continued on and finally walked upon the abbey's granges.

Head bowed low, he repeated the name Stephen to himself in a whisper three times. Had his parents chosen that name the same way Brother Andrew had picked "Alexander"?

"Stephen is an honorable name," the monk said, watching him closely.

He looked up in a daze. "*My* name?"

"Aye. Stephen was a great man; a courageous Christian; a beloved saint—the first to give his life for the faith. The early Christians were persecuted, but Saint Stephen did not fear. In the end, an angry mob stoned him to death, and his soul rose up to Heaven. Our first martyr."

Maybe that was his true identity—a martyr. Yet, without his memory, his real name sounded even more foreign than the one the monk had made up for him.

The boys' dormitory came into sight, but he stopped abruptly. "Brother—?"

"Aye, my son."

"May I . . . may I be called Xan a while longer?"

The monk put his hand on the boy's shoulder and gave a warm smile. "I understand. Of course you may. And tomorrow we will spend some time discussing what to do about your future—Xan."

Suffering

The next morning came too quickly. He'd arrived back after all the boys were sleeping and now woke to the light of dawn peeking through a slit in the dorm window—his first day as a true orphan.

How strange to realize he had no family to search for today, no reason to jump off the straw mattress in anticipation of all the day might bring. He already knew what to expect: chores and bullying and playing games he'd forgotten.

Perhaps it was better to have no memory. That way he couldn't remember all he'd lost.

Brother Leo opened the door to the upper room and rang an obnoxious bell to wake them. There would be morning prayers and then chore assignments and then breakfast in the refectory and then work and then play time. This was to be his life now.

Morning prayers passed—had he even heard the words?—and then they gathered in front of the dorm to receive their daily work. Brother Leo made the assignments, giving Xan the job to scrub the stones on the fountain in the circle. Some of the boys groaned at the long list of chores.

"Today is the final day of my week with you," Brother Leo announced.

That was the only bit of good news Xan had received in this new life of his.

"Brother Oscar will be here at days' end to start his week of supervision," the monk said. "As you can see, I have assigned you extra work to keep you busy in my absence today."

"Where are you going?" Joshua asked.

"I must tend to my duties as a cellarer."

Being a cellarer was an important job. Brother Andrew had explained the other day that cellarers made sure the abbey had all the food and other items it needed to function.

"And did you not hear," Brother Leo continued, "the abbot recently appointed me to manage Penwood Manor? I must travel there today to ensure they are fulfilling their harvest goals."

Penwood was the manor that Lord Godfrey had got so upset about yesterday.

After Brother Leo left, Xan took a small metal pail and a wire brush to the ring of bushes on the meadow with the fountain at its center. The striped fish swam in circles under the murky water. To those fish, every day was exactly the same, just like Xan's life would be now.

He scrubbed at the lowest, flattest stone on the outside of the fountain. Bits of green moss gave way beneath the strength of the wire brush that he'd dunked into the pail of water.

If only the great weight upon his soul could be so easily chipped away.

His parents had been murdered at the hands of bandits. He himself had been left for dead by that brutal scarred man. Maybe they were all cursed, just as Old Tom had said.

"You're still here." A soft voice approached from behind. It was Lucy.

He spun around. There she was, walking with Sister Regina, who was dressed in black cloth from the tip of her head to the heel of her boots. The nun wore a large crucifix; a wisp of golden hair stuck out from the edge of her habit, brushing against the dimple on her rosy cheek.

"Good dawning," she said. "I am Sister Regina. Lucy has told me all about you."

Xan stood and gave a half-wave. "Good morn."

"Sister and I were enjoying some fresh air and decided to visit the fish," Lucy said, her hair gleaming in the morning light even blacker than the nun's habit. "The monks always draw a few from the fishpond and place them in the fountain 'til winter comes."

"They're swimming around in there, same as always," he said.

The three of them sat on the ledge and stared into the water.

"I thought you'd be in Chadwick with your family by now," Lucy said.

Xan gave a deep sigh and told them about yesterday's events. When he'd finished, Lucy's brown eyes were glistening, and even the nun was pressing her sleeve to her cheeks.

"I'm so sorry, Xan," Lucy said. "I'll say all my prayers today for you and your family."

That was a sweet offer. His prayers for his parents had not brought them back to him, yet maybe Lucy's prayers would combine with Brother Andrew's to let his family rest in peace.

"I understand how alone you must feel right now," Sister Regina said.

He peered into her eyes—green and sorrowful. She seemed moved by his story, but no one could truly understand how he felt. How could they?

"I too lost my family when I was young," the nun said, her voice trembling. "A plague swept through my village. I will not speak of it, except to say that in one week I lost my mother, my father, and even my little sister, Eva."

Pressure grew within Xan's chest. "How old were you?" he asked.

"Fourteen."

He nodded. Maybe this woman *could* understand. She too had lost everything, and she had felt her loss in full. Xan was spared at least that—knowing he was alone but not remembering how much he'd loved his parents or all the things he must live without now that they were gone.

"How did you carry on without them?" he asked.

The nun grasped the wooden crucifix on her robe. She pointed at it: Jesus nailed to a cross, an anguished expression on his face.

"I saw how our Lord Jesus suffered for me. Then I knew I was not alone; that God understood my pain. Now, I have God as my father, Jesus as my brother, and Mary as my mother."

Xan gazed at the crucifix. The crown of thorns encircled the crucified man's head like a monk's tonsure. Truly the man lay in misery upon it.

"The Lord helped me bear my burdens," Sister Regina said. "And over time, true faith and joy were born in my heart, but only after a great labor of confusion and doubt."

Xan bowed his head low but said nothing. Was the path the nun took to find happiness the only way? It sounded much too painful.

A long moment passed as all three of them watched the striped fish in the hazy pool.

"When Father left me here at the convent, I felt so miserable," Lucy said. "Then one day I asked Sister Cecilia to teach me to play the harp and I started to feel better. Do you see?"

The girl's sad expression had been replaced by a peaceful look.

"You think I should learn to play the harp to make me feel better?" Xan said.

Lucy shook her head. "That's not what I meant at all." The little mole on her cheek turned down with her lips. "Find something to learn; some purpose here. That's what I mean."

Sister Regina nodded. "Lucy has a point. If you find your purpose—where you fit into this new life of yours—then you will find your joy again. And perhaps your memory too."

"Have you found your purpose here?" Xan asked Brother Andrew later that day, after he'd finished his chores and the sun had begun to set below the woodland.

They walked together in the granges, talking about what had happened yesterday.

"I believe so," the monk said. "At least I am on my way to fulfilling my purpose. 'Tis my life's desire to become a priest one day."

Brother Andrew had explained that priests were monks who could do special jobs, such as leading the Mass and even forgiving sins through a Sacrament called Confession.

"Do all monks become priests?"

"Nay. Look at Brother Leo. He has lived at this abbey most of his adult years and has thrice refused the chance to become a priest. He sees a different purpose for his life."

Xan stared at his callused hands again. As a peasant from Hardonbury, his purpose might be to labor in the granges like the abbey's servants and lay brothers. Yet Brother Andrew seemed to think differently.

"What do *you* think is my purpose here?" he asked.

The monk stopped walking and turned to face him. "I have been praying about that very thing, and I have a question to ask. You have traveled to Hardonbury and Chadwick. How many of those peasants do you think are lettered?"

The old woman and Old Tom hadn't seemed educated. Nor had the guards and many of the others he'd seen as they'd journeyed. "I don't know, Brother. Not many, I suppose."

"Maybe none. Nobles teach their children, and we monks must be lettered, of course. If not for us, the ancient works from Greece and

Rome would be lost to the world, along with the Holy Scriptures. We read them; interpret them; recopy them. Perhaps you too could be lettered."

"But I'm just a peasant from Hardonbury. Look at my hands." He raised them high.

The monk pushed Xan's hands down. "Some of our novices also come from peasant families. I have observed you these past few days. God has given you a mind for learning. Your questions are thoughtful and curious. Your insight is as good as any pupil I have taught."

"You think I should become a novice monk?"

"That is for God to say, not me. Our abbot would make you wait at least a year ere allowing it, anyhow. But if you wish, I could take you as my own pupil. Would you like that?"

"Aye, Brother."

This might be what Lucy meant. If he learned to read and write, as she'd learned the harp, maybe he could tolerate this life. But could he ever understand his pain, like Sister Regina understood hers?

"There's something I don't understand, Brother." He told the monk about the nun's story.

Brother Andrew nodded as though he knew its meaning. "Sister tells of the great sorrows Jesus bore for us all. The Lord can take our pain and use it for a good purpose—even to heal."

"To heal what?"

"To heal the damage caused by sin. God can work inside our hearts and—"

A low rumble vibrated the granges. The tremor started as a tickle in Xan's shoes but soon grew stronger. A thundering sound echoed from the edge of the woodland.

"What's that?" Xan said.

Brother Andrew paused to listen. "'Tis the galloping of many horses. And the clamor draws nearer."

The sun had already set, and twilight had begun to cover the land. Why would the abbey get a host of visitors at this hour?

Just then, a light flashed in Xan's mind: a vision of a man rising in dim light from a mattress, his hair in shambles, his face lined with worry, a woman by his side. Somehow, Xan knew the man was Father and the woman was Mother.

This was another memory: the moment disaster had come to Hardonbury Manor.

"Could it be bandits?" Xan said.

The monk jumped to his feet. "Whose horses would come in the night like this?"

One of the sheepdogs barked in the distance, soon joined by the howling of others.

"Jude's folly!" Brother Andrew shouted. "You could be right. Stay here."

With that, the monk raced toward the abbey shouting, "Toll the bells!"

Bandits

The bells rang across the abbey grounds—*clang, clang, clang*! Their urgency jarred the injury that had been healing on Xan's head, causing it to ache like it hadn't done for days.

The thundering sound of the hooves had peaked and then begun to recede, replaced by screams and shouts and whooping voices in the night. Darkness had fallen upon the granges, with Xan standing alone near the rows of wheat, unable to see much of anything.

Suddenly a light arose—a flame and smoke coming from somewhere on the abbey's grounds. Were the bandits setting the monastery on fire? Surely the monks had done nothing to deserve this, but neither had his parents in Hardonbury.

Brother Andrew had told him to wait in the granges, but something was urging him to follow the monk—something in his memories. With each returning vision, he seemed to see the other memories that had returned all the more clearly in his mind.

There sat the scarred bandit on his horse, staring down at the men of Hardonbury. One of those with a shovel was the man on the mattress with the messy hair and the worried look—Father. But how had that bandit murdered Father and also chased Xan far into the wood-land? And why?

The hooting and crying grew louder from the main abbey complex. Should he stay or go?

Maybe he'd fled Hardonbury the day of the attack like a coward, leaving his family to die. Or he might have done something brave that day—aye, it must be so—something to make the scarred man angry enough to chase him such a long distance.

No matter. Whether he'd been a coward or a hero in Hardonbury, he wouldn't stand by now and watch these kind monks be hurt without raising a hand to defend them.

He sprinted across the granges toward the abbey grounds. He rushed through the gate that led to the cobblestone path, following it until he neared the abbot's tiny house.

The firelight was brighter now, dim and foggy like the moments before a red dawn.

At that instant, a tall man in a chain-mail shirt stepped from the abbot's quarters holding an iron sword in a black-gloved hand. His face was older, with deep wrinkles and a pointy silver beard. Around his neck was a dragon pendant. This must be a bandit!

Xan ducked around the corner of a wooden supply shed, where he could still see.

A second bandit, dressed in a black shirt and pants and carrying a torch, ran up to the older one. "Was the abbot in his quarters, Carlo?"

The one with the sword—Carlo—shook his head. "Nay. Did you search the main church?"

"He is not there either," the man in black said. "Why is it so impor-tant that we find him?"

Carlo stuck the sword toward the other bandit. "That is *my* business. Your business is to follow my orders and collect your reward."

"Aye, Carlo," he said. He took the torch and shoved it onto the wooden roof of the abbot's house. In a moment, the flames would set it ablaze.

"Stop!" Carlo shouted. "What are you doing? I said to strike and steal, not kill and destroy. We will not spill innocent blood without need in this holy place. Only the abbot will see harm."

The two bandits marched up the cobblestone path toward the chapter house.

Xan crept out from behind the shed and followed them.

These bandits were here for the abbot, but why? Carlo, who acted like their leader, seemed to have specific instructions. And some kind of reward would be given, but from whom?

He followed the bandits past the chapter house. Outside the eight-sided building, a shrubbery burned brightly. Other bandits—possibly a dozen of them—bustled in and out of other structures, probably looking for the abbot. The monks must have all gone into hiding.

The two bandits strode past the monks' dormitory. The wavering voice of an elderly monk yelled out from within the dorm, maybe at a different bandit inside: "Stop, servant of evil!"

Xan picked up a stone from the path. How nicely it fit in his palm; how comfortable and familiar. Had he done this before? When he was rescuing Lucy from the boys, he'd had a similar urge to throw a stone at John.

He abandoned following Carlo and the other bandit, stepping instead through a side door into the monks' dorm. Inside, a grunt and a crash rang out.

The elderly monk—Father Paul, who had been in the refectory at breakfast yesterday—lay upon the floor. A tall bandit in black stood over him with a studded mace in hand, ready to strike.

The monk suddenly reached for the bandit's waist, grasping the leather pouch on his belt. It tore open. Coins scattered everywhere. A crumpled parchment dropped to the stone floor.

Father Paul grabbed up the parchment and clenched it tightly as the bandit ripped most of it from his hand. The bandit raised the mace again to strike. He would probably kill the poor priest.

Xan flung the stone at the bandit. It missed, striking the wall directly in front of him.

The man turned his eyes toward Xan, revealing a jagged scar and a crooked nose. It was the man from his visions—the one on horseback; the one who'd raised the mace to murder him.

The bandit recoiled in surprise. "You, boy? I thought I *killed* you!"

This was definitely that bandit. The last time he'd seen him, the man had chased him relentlessly into the woodland. Surely the bandit would try to finish the job now at any cost.

Xan turned and fled.

By running away, he might actually save Father Paul's life. That bandit's face had been filled with rage, like the beast from his dream with eyes of speckled red and a hideous, malformed snout. The man would pursue him and leave the priest on the stone floor.

But how would Xan escape? His head throbbed; his legs ached; his heart thumped.

He needed to hide.

"Come back here, boy!" the scarred man yelled, rushing from the monks' dorm after him.

Fires were springing up all over the abbey grounds. Xan sprinted past a burning shrub and a wooden wagon that had been set aflame on one side.

That's it!

He circled back and dove under the blazing wagon, curling up under the side that was not in flames. The bandit might not suspect that he'd choose such a risky hiding place. The heat would be bearable, at least for a little while.

Sure enough, the bandit sprinted past the wagon and ran directly into his leader.

"Rummy, what are you doing?" Carlo shouted, pushing the scarred man away.

"That boy from the village! He is still alive."

Carlo pointed his broad sword in Rummy's face. "Enough! Sound the retreat."

Rummy didn't move. "I will not let that boy escape again."

Carlo glared at him. "Enough, you fool! He is just a boy. We must go."

A long moment passed. Finally Rummy obeyed. He whistled with his fingers in the sides of his mouth, piercing the air three times with a signal.

Then Carlo and Rummy headed up the path.

Xan crawled from under the wagon, away from the ever-increasing heat.

First things first—he must check on Father Paul. If Rummy had hit him with a mace, the old priest would need serious care from the abbey's leech, Brother Lucius.

He rushed to the monks' dorm. Father Paul was gone. Maybe someone had helped him.

What next? Lucy and Joshua. Who would protect them?

"Please, God," he breathed. "You can do anything. At least keep Lucy safe."

He exited the dorm. It would take five minutes to get to the convent running at full pace.

Another whistle screeched. Two bandits jogged up the path in the direction Carlo had gone.

They passed Xan without a second look. That probably meant the bandits were gathering to leave.

He ran.

There, ahead in the distance, past the granges, someone had just set fire to the hedge near the trail that led to Chadwick. Some of the bandits must have invaded the boys' dormitory and convent! Perhaps they hadn't heard Rummy's whistle at that distance.

Xan ran faster, out the gate and into the wheat, ignoring the pain in his head. He crossed the granges, climbed the grassy hill, and looked back. Several small fires were lighting up the night around the main abbey structures.

Just then, voices rose from the bottom of the hill. Two figures stood on the convent path.

"Why are you wandering out here?" A man's voice—Brother Andrew. "'Tis not safe."

"I just wanted to make sure everything was all right." That was Lucy! Xan rushed down the hill.

Grunts echoed from along the convent path, heading toward them. Two more figures—far too tall to be nuns—were jogging up the trail.

"I tell ya that I heard Rummy's signal," one of them said. "Clear as day."

Xan reached the bottom of the hill, stumbling to a stop before Lucy and the monk.

"Xan!" Lucy said. The dim light from the hedge lit up her eyes.

"Praise God, you are safe!" Brother Andrew cried. "Where did you go? I have been searching all over for you. Quickly, both of you—get to the boys' dormitory. Someone is coming."

Too late. The bandits had seen them.

"Hey, you!" The men charged toward them.

Brother Andrew stepped into the path, blocking Lucy and Xan from the bandits.

Xan dropped to the dirt, reaching all around. If he could just find a rock to throw.

"Get out of our way, ya dumb monk!" The lead bandit pushed Brother Andrew hard. The monk fell backward into Lucy, and both of them tumbled to the grass.

In the dimness, the lead bandit must not have seen Xan, still crouching on the path looking for a stone. He tripped over Xan's body and fell to the trail on his face, crying out in pain.

Xan dove for the grass before the second bandit's foot could kick him in the head.

"Get up, Rolf, you simpkin," the second bandit said.

Another whistle sounded—this one in three short bursts.

"Like I told you," he said. "The signal. Now c'mon, ere they leave without us."

The two bandits doubled their pace up the hill as Xan jumped to his feet.

Brother Andrew helped Lucy rise. "Xan, take this girl back to the convent. Then round up all the boys and meet me at the abbey church. We will need every spare hand tonight."

The monk took to the path in the direction the bandits had gone.

"Are you all right?" Xan asked her.

Lucy nodded. "You really got that bandit bad. He probably scraped his whole face."

"Good. Come on, let's get you back to the convent."

They hurried down the convent path. Now that the hedge fire had burned itself out, darkness covered them completely.

"Are we still on the path?" she said. "I can't even see my feet."

A warm, soft hand pressed on his forearm, working its way down to his callused fingers. She'd taken his hand in the dark for support as they walked the final stretch.

His memory reached back only about a week, but holding Lucy's hand at that moment surely must have been the finest, most exhilarating feeling ever. The pains and bruises on his body were instantly gone. Boundless energy flowed through his tired legs.

The convent door opened. Sister Regina appeared in the crack with a candle.

Lucy released his hand with a gentle squeeze and hurried to the nun.

"Where have you been?" Sister Regina said. "I have been worried sick."

Lucy gave Xan a wave and a splendid smile. Then she disappeared inside with the nun.

He stood alone on the path, quite warm despite the chill breeze in his face.

"Enough, Xan; move it," he whispered to himself. Brother Andrew still needed help.

He raced back to the boys' dormitory, but it was empty. Perhaps Brother Oscar or Brother Leo had arrived and already led the boys to the abbey.

Back he ran, over the granges and onto the cobblestone path. He coughed from the smoke. All around, small fires—more dangerous than any bandit—threatened the abbey's structures.

Memory or not, he knew someone needed to get water on those fires, or the abbey would be destroyed. The wood cottages of Hardonbury must have caught fire much worse than these stone abbey buildings. Maybe Rummy hadn't killed his parents after all—perhaps the fire did it.

He passed the main church and peeked inside. Someone in there might help. The prior stood within, gently holding a wooden box and commanding several monks cleaning up the debris.

The prior's belly shook under his robe as he shouted. "They looted the sacristy and stole the chalices." He held the box high. "And look, the fiends even desecrated the Blessed Sacrament!"

Brother Andrew had said the holy bread of the Blessed Sacrament was the very presence of Christ to them. No wonder the prior was so upset—definitely in no condition to put out fires.

Xan stepped outside. Voices were yelling around the corner. He followed the sounds.

Near the refectory, servants had piped in water from the fishpond. Brother Andrew was lining up the novices and younger boys to pass buckets of water to douse the fires.

"There you are, Xan!" the monk said. "Hurry. We need your hands."

Just then, the abbot turned the corner.

Xan had never actually met the abbot, but he'd seen him in the distance, and this was definitely him. He was shorter and frailer than his reputation. His bald head had mostly lost its hair, except for a faint ring of gray that must have been a tonsure at one time. Yet his hands were large and beefy, as though he'd worked his life threshing wheat.

The abbot yawned and rubbed his eyes. Perhaps he'd been sleeping and was still stuck in a dream. He gazed about before he finally spoke. "What has happened? Where is the prior?"

Brother Andrew rushed over and embraced the old abbot. "Praise God, you are alive! We thought the bandits might have taken you. Where have you been?"

"Praying in our dormitory chapel, as I always do after *compline*." He turned in a circle, fires all about him. "Why are you all just standing there? Get water on these fires."

Joshua hurried over to Xan and pulled at his tunic. "You can work with me," the boy said, the fire lighting up his freckles like glowing embers on his cheeks.

Xan grabbed a bucket of water. "Thanks, Joshua. Follow me."

13

Purpose

The next morning, the boys slept late. They'd stayed up most of the night to help fight the fires, until each threat had been fully doused. Half the fishpond had been emptied in the process.

Then Brother Oscar had escorted them back to the dorm—the first day of his turn watching the boys.

In those final hours, Xan had learned that Father Paul had survived his fight with Rummy, though he was in the infirmary recovering from his wounds. As for the abbot, when he'd returned from *compline*—the monks' evening prayers—the elderly man had fallen asleep in the tiny chapel tucked away in the monks' dorm. Had he come out during the attack, Carlo would have hurt him.

Xan awoke before the other boys and found Brother Andrew exiting the main abbey church, where the monks had just finished *terce*, their mid-morning prayers.

"I am glad to see you," the monk said, his brown and blue eyes now set within dark rings of sleeplessness. "I want to tell you how brave and hard-working you were last night."

"Thank you, Brother." Except this wasn't the time for rewards. Last night, he hadn't the chance to do anything except put out fires. He still must tell the monk what he'd seen and heard.

"May I speak to you for a moment?"

"Of course." He led them to a stone bench nearby, where Xan began his story.

As soon as he mentioned Carlo's purpose to harm the abbot, Brother Andrew interrupted. "No more, Xan. These are serious words you speak. You must tell them to the abbot."

The monk took him to the chapter house, with its sharply pointed roof. Voices spoke urgently within. Brother Andrew knocked on the door and then entered with Xan.

Inside, the abbot was meeting with the prior and Brother Leo around a wide, wooden table surrounded by thick chairs. "We *must* ask Lord Godfrey for help," Brother Leo was urging.

As soon as the monks saw Xan, they stopped talking and gawked at him. Maybe they didn't want to discuss abbey business in front of a peasant boy, but surely they'd make an exception for him this one time. He'd taken action last night; he'd seen and heard important things.

"I am sorry to interrupt, Abbot," Brother Andrew said, "but this boy has urgent news."

They sat Xan at the table and listened to his account of events and of his memories. Their eyes widened as he spoke. By the time he'd finished, their demeanor had changed toward him.

"What a remarkable boy," the abbot said. "Surely our Lord has a mighty purpose for you."

But Brother Leo poked a purply finger in the air. "What this boy says only makes my argument stronger. Last night, those bandits burned our manor house at Penwood, then rode here to harm our abbot. Our nuns and children are at the mercy of these men without Godfrey's help."

What terrible news! Had Brother Leo been at Penwood when the bandits had attacked there? He hadn't been around for the fires at the abbey. Perhaps he'd arrived late from his journey.

"But Leo," the prior said. "Godfrey will not defend us 'til the abbot admits Godfrey's claim over Penwood. Have you forgotten how, just last year, Godfrey threatened us with suit in the courts?"

Brother Leo snorted. "I manage Penwood now, and I can tell you the people there are terrified. Father Paul is wounded; our abbot is threatened. Cursed times call for new decisions."

Had Xan's news added to all this trouble? Maybe he should have kept it to himself.

The prior pulled at the graying beard on his chin. "Nay, Leo. If we give Penwood Manor to Godfrey, as you suggest, what will he want from us next—Oakwood Manor? The abbey itself?"

"Enough!" The abbot raised a hefty hand. "King Henry has fought against our Church for far too long. He wants power to control our bishops, priests, and everyone else. I will not turn over our dear Penwood Manor to one of the King's men, no matter how noble Lord Godfrey might be."

The abbot glanced in Xan's direction. The monk must hate that this kind of disagreement would be aired in front of a peasant boy. Yet Brother Leo hadn't finished being grumpy.

"Not everyone agrees with you, Abbot," he said, raising his voice. "Last night—"

The abbot slammed his hand to the table. "Not another word, Brother Leo, or your discipline shall be severe! If you are concerned for this abbey's safety, I suggest you meditate on the Psalms: 'tis the Lord who is our Shepherd and Protector, *not* Lord Godfrey."

The room grew awkwardly quiet. Brother Leo bowed his head, though his face was red and sweaty and his eyebrows stood on edge.

Xan's parents and so many others had been killed by the bandits. These men were so evil they had even desecrated the holy bread in the church. Brother Leo might be right about needing help from Lord

Godfrey. Last night, most of the monks had hidden from the danger. If the bandits came again, who would protect the boys and the nuns, and Lucy?

God might be able to do anything, but all the praying of the monks hadn't stopped the bandits from coming. If Carlo wanted to kill the abbot, what would stop him from returning?

"Are there other matters to discuss?" the abbot said.

Silence.

"Good," he said. "There is much to clean after last night's disaster. Let us get to it."

Xan reported back to the boys' dormitory. As the abbot had said, the abbey was a complete shambles. That meant Brother Oscar would be assigning lots of extra work for the boys.

Their new dorm-keeper shared many unfortunate traits with Brother Leo, including a love of yelling. Though not as old as Leo, Brother Oscar had graying hair that also refused to cooperate. A clumpy ball of hair stuck up on one side of his head, so that his ringed tonsure looked pregnant.

The monk gathered the boys on the grass outside the dorm and assigned them chores. He told Xan to pick up every scrap of debris and ash that had floated over from the fires at the main abbey to anywhere in the meadow, from the fountain to the convent path.

After the monk withdrew inside, Joshua meandered over with a frown. "Why do I always have to sweep the floors?" he whined, scratching at his red hair, still black with ash.

Before Xan could answer, John approached in a huff, his fingernails caked with grime. "Well, I bet you think you're someone important now, don't you, Sire Clumsy?"

Of all days, why would that bully start trouble today? John must realize the miserable week he'd had: learning about his family, being trapped at this abbey, surviving the bandits' attack.

"What are you talking about?" Xan said, as the other boys gathered around.

"I saw you last night and this morning, all friendly with the monks." John rolled his eyes. "Now that you're stuck here, you want to be the monks' little pet, eh? Hoping for better chores and bigger helpings at breakfast, probably."

Could it be possible that John was jealous of him, even after all his troubles? John's family had probably died in that plague last year. Perhaps he was as miserable as Xan. Or worse.

"John, just leave me alone and do your work. I'm in no mood for this." He turned to leave.

John grabbed Xan's shoulders from behind and threw him to the ground.

"Don't tell me what to do, clumsy," John said, towering over him.

Xan stumbled to his feet as the boys circled round: "Fight! Fight! Fight!"

Joshua—eyes filled with alarm—ran into the dormitory.

Xan stood his ground. Rummy's evil face filled his mind—sneering down at Father, staring at Father Paul with hateful red eyes. That feeling of rage returned. He lifted his fists.

John pounced, knocking him to the ground, punching at his side. All he could do was protect his face from the blows. Finally he rolled out and sprang up—lip bleeding, side aching.

John would attack again; it was as certain as wheat growing in the granges each season.

Sure enough, the bully threw another wild fist in the air. This time Xan was ready.

As John swung, Xan tripped up the bully's legs. John's fist flailed through the air; his legs collapsed under him; his backside crashed to the ground, followed by his shoulders and head. He looked so awkward falling to the grass that a few of the boys even laughed aloud.

A deep voice suddenly boomed from the window above: "Stop, or I will put the paddle to you both!"—Brother Oscar. Joshua must have told him about the fight.

John stared up and then put his fists down. Maybe he was remembering that paddling from Brother Leo the other day. One public paddling might have been enough for him.

"We'll finish this later," he promised as he stomped off, followed by a couple of the boys.

Xan licked the bitter blood from his lips.

The others had scattered in fear to do their chores. He might as well get to work too.

He started at the fountain and picked his way across the meadow, putting all the debris in a large wooden crate. At least he'd have time to think without bullies or angry monks around.

Lucy had told him to find a purpose, and Brother Andrew had offered to teach him his letters, just like the novice boys. That's what the monk wanted, no doubt—for Xan to become a novice one day. Then he'd take the vow of stability and be at the abbey forever.

Learning to read and write would be interesting, but would it be a purpose? The faces of Mother and Father were growing clearer each day. Mother's eyes were as gentle as Lucy's, but she never did much of anything in his visions except look at him. Yet even her gaze made him want to cry for some reason. Other memories might come soon, even harder to deal with.

Nay, being lettered might be a good goal, but it wouldn't change anything. It wouldn't explain why he'd lost his family or why the monks were being threatened. It wouldn't even discredit those frightening stories of the Shadow that John liked to tell.

By the time Xan had worked his way to the convent path, the midday sun sparkled overhead. Maybe the girls were down there cleaning the convent yard from the bandits' attack.

He looked at the hand Lucy had held last night. It still felt warm. Why not go see her?

He wandered along the trail, checking behind him for Brother Oscar. Several of the younger girls were outside playing with dolls made from old rags. They watched him go by.

He arrived at the convent door. He knocked. What would he say? The nuns might get mad at him for trying to meet with Lucy. Maybe he could pretend to be lost—nay, that would be dotie.

The door opened. Sister Regina stood there, surprised. "Xan, what are you doing here?"

"Good day, Sister."

She noticed his fresh scrapes and bruises. "Oh, my. Have you been fighting?"

"I'm fine. I was just checking to see if everything was all right here after last night."

"The Lord protected us," the nun said, smiling as if she knew Xan's real reason for coming.

She glanced over her shoulder as another nun passed by. "Lucy told me about you tripping that bandit. I wish I could invite you in to check on her, but the rules do not allow it." Then she lowered her voice. "Take the cobbled path and go around back. We will meet you there."

He followed her direction and took the path to an empty, tidy garden without flowers or people. It likely would bloom in a burst of colors in the springtime.

He sat on a stone wall and waited.

"Hello again," Lucy said, stepping out the back door with Sister Regina. She was dressed as always in a flowing white tunic, cinched at her waist by a slim brown belt.

"Sister says you've been fighting." She came and sat next to him while the nun crossed to the far side of the garden and picked dead leaves from a tall plant.

They spoke for a while about the situation with John. Then he told her about Brother Andrew's offer to teach him to read and write.

"That's exactly what you need, Xan. You'll start feeling better ere you know it."

He shrugged. "I don't know about that. Especially not after last night." He told her about all he'd seen of Carlo and Rummy, and about the monks' angry meeting this morning.

"How dreadful," she said. "Why would anyone want to hurt the abbot?"

"I don't know."

It was a mystery. The same bandits who had killed his family and destroyed his home were now terrorizing the good monks at this abbey. None of it made sense.

That's it!

The idea came in a flash. How could he not have thought of it before?

"Lucy, I think I might know why God sent me to this abbey, and what I need to do now."

Her eyes grew wide with anticipation. "You do?"

He stood. "I think I'm the one who's supposed to solve the mystery of these bandits. And when I do, I'll finally understand why all this has happened to me and my family."

14

Discovery

That night the rains came again, heavy and cold, and continued into the next morning, carrying away the ashes and washing black stains from the stone buildings.

Brother Oscar gave only indoor chores to the boys, putting them to work throughout the abbey's buildings. The monk assigned Xan and John work on opposite sides of the abbey grounds. That was fine with Xan, although John had not spoken a word to him since their fight yesterday.

In the afternoon, Brother Andrew escorted Xan across the wet meadow and granges to the abbey's library for his first lesson as the monk's pupil.

"You will learn to love the library—a quiet place in troubled times," the monk said. "'Twill be your place to learn, much like the school-room where novices are taught by our novice master."

Grasping the large handle, Brother Andrew opened the creaking door and led him into a plain room with a large, wooden table, two chairs, and four tall shelves filled with leather-bound books. Its most striking feature was an enormous painting on the back wall, visible upon entry.

"What is *that*?" Xan said, pointing.

The painting was disturbing. In it, a man's bloody body lay dead on the ground, eyes closed but lips turned up in a smile. A semblance of the man's soul rose from his body. The soul—almost transparent, with a yellow halo circling its head—had its eyes open and wore a peaceful expression. The soul seemed to stare down from the painting, its eyes meeting and holding Xan's gaze.

Brother Andrew looked at him with concern. "Do not be afraid, my son."

It seemed that everywhere he'd turned since his injury, death was present—in his dreams, in the stories of the boys, in Hardonbury and Chadwick, and now even in this library.

"Why would someone paint this poor man's death?" he asked.

The monk pondered a moment. "Death is our companion. Wars, plagues—there is much death these days. By displaying it in art, we understand death better. That is why I painted this."

"*You* painted this?"

"Indeed. I was well schooled in the art as a child. But 'tis not meant to frighten. That man is Saint Ignatius of Antioch, an early martyr for the faith."

"Well," Xan said. "When I die, I don't think I'll be smiling."

The monk chuckled. "When our Lord died on the cross, He conquered death. That is the beauty of our faith. Death is a gateway to Heaven, and I hope to welcome mine one day as Saint Ignatius is doing here. He does not fear his death, you see."

The saint in the painting showed no sign of terror; it was like Mother's face in his dream, when she let Death in through the cottage door. Maybe Mother was a person of great faith too.

He stared at the painting again. The monk's words sounded nice, yet hadn't the monks hidden in fear from the bandits? Not Brother Andrew, though. He'd run toward the danger.

"Now," the monk said. "Let us begin."

He sat Xan at the table and placed a piece of goat-skin parchment in front of him.

"First, you must learn your letters, Xan. Then you will see that these letters can form words in the two languages you must master: Latin and our common tongue here in England."

The monk picked up a pointed stylus that had been whittled smooth from a reed. He dipped it into a tiny, foul-smelling cup of ink—made from iron and the gall of an oak tree, he'd said—and scrawled a black letter on the rough parchment, commenting on how to shape the letter properly and what it sounded like in both English and Latin.

"This is how we monks have preserved the Sacred Scriptures and great works of antiquity. A practiced monk who spends his days in the scriptorium becomes expert in writing these letters."

Eventually the page was filled with all the letters Xan needed to learn.

"Our youngest monks make the best scribes," Brother Andrew said. "When a monk's eyes get too old, like with Brother Leo or Brother Oscar, copying manuscripts becomes too difficult."

After two hours of tedious work, going through each of the letters, Xan's mind felt fuller than the fountain had been this morning, nearly overflowing from all the rain.

Brother Andrew stood. "Excellent work, my son. You have done as well as any novice boy." He placed the parchment to the side. "I will leave this here for you to use each day. The abbot has given permission for you to come to the library to study during any of your free time."

It would probably take Xan days to memorize the look and sound of each of these letters. Writing them perfectly would be even more difficult. But all these letters could not get him closer to his true purpose for being at the abbey.

"Brother," he said, as the monk put the ink on a shelf. "I think I might know why God has brought me to this place."

"Is that so?" Brother Andrew stopped immediately and turned to him.

He told the monk his idea that no coincidence had brought a boy from Hardonbury to this abbey just when the same group of bandits had attacked both places. He explained his hope that, by solving the mystery, he might understand his situation and perhaps even find his memories.

"Remarkable," Brother Andrew said. "I feel in my heart that you are correct about this."

The monk stepped to one of the shelves and pulled a thick, leather-bound book down to the table. He opened its stinky leaves of parchment and paged through it.

"This book records a history of our shire, prepared over the years by our archivists. I often consult it for research on matters involving local manors. Perhaps you will discover something of importance in here about Hardonbury or the abbey, once you begin to read."

Xan inspected the book. None of the words on the pages made sense yet, though some of the letters already looked familiar after just one lesson. Perhaps reading really *would* be helpful in figuring out the mystery of why his parents had been killed at the hands of the bandits.

He flipped a few leaves, glancing at the words and diagrams within. Several line drawings were labeled. One set of sketches appeared to show Harwood Abbey at different stages of its construction. The book even contained an old map of the local area.

He had nearly lost interest when he flipped the next page. There lay a drawing of a shield engraved with two swords that crossed together over images of a serpent and a cross. That was the same image Sire Roger had shown them on the tapestry at Lord Godfrey's estate.

"What does this say, Brother?"

The monk squinted to read the words. The ink had been blotted on the rough page, which still contained some goat hair on the parchment skin. The ink blot obscured some of the letters.

"Of course," Brother Andrew said. "This section of the book sets out the history of Chadwick Manor. Here is the coat of arms for the Godfrey family—we saw it on that tapestry inside his manor house, you might recall. It says here that our archivist copied this drawing from a wax seal placed on an official document signed by Lord Godfrey in 1174."

A wax seal. Aye, Sire Roger had mentioned that to them.

Brother Andrew closed the book and placed it on the table. "Come, Xan. See, the sun is finally shining. Let us go warm ourselves in its light."

They exited the library and strode down a long hallway and out the back door. Sure enough, the rains had finally gone, and the sun was high and bright in the sky.

A tall servant in a brown tunic passed by, marching toward the abbey gate. He carried a crossbow in hand, with a quiver of quarrels on his back. A hairy brown dog walked by his side.

Brother Andrew nodded in approval. "The abbot has asked three of our servants who can use the crossbow to guard our gates in case those bandits come back."

In one of Xan's memories, Rummy was sneering down at a group of the Hardonbury men—Father included—trying to defend Hardonbury from attack. Those poor men had failed, so what could three servants with bows do to protect the abbey if the bandits returned with a vengeance?

"And look, your new friend is coming," the monk said, pointing at the cobblestone path.

Two girls approached carrying a hefty, folded blanket. It was Lucy and a shorter girl—the same one who had delivered linens with Lucy the day Xan had met her. The younger girl wore a long brown tunic and had bushy eyebrows like caterpillars.

Lucy smiled and waved as they drew near. Her hair seemed flatter and smoother than usual. Maybe she'd been caught in the rain earlier. It didn't matter; she looked just as pretty either way.

"Good day, Brother Andrew; Xan." Lucy curtsied politely. "The sun is finally out."

"Praise God for that," the monk said.

"Hullo!" The younger girl's long brown hair toppled over her face as she curtsied.

"This is Maud," Lucy said.

They all exchanged greetings.

"Sister said to bring this here blanket for poor ol' Father Paul," Maud said.

"Is he still in the infirmary?" Lucy asked.

"Aye, he is still recovering there," the monk said. "And with all these cold rains, he could use an extra blanket. That was very kind of the sisters to think of him. Xan, would you show these girls to the infirmary, please? I must return to my duties in the scriptorium."

Brother Andrew had given him the perfect excuse to walk with them. Had the monk done that on purpose, or was he really in that much of a rush to get back to writing with smelly ink?

After Brother Andrew had gone, Xan led the girls to the edge of the monks' dormitory, where they entered and headed toward the infirmary.

"'Tis good to see you," he said to Lucy as they walked.

She smiled, and her cheek turned red. "Maud has been a great helper with the deliveries today," she said.

"I'm always the best helper," Maud confirmed.

When they got to the infirmary, Father Paul was sitting up in bed, speaking with the abbey's leech, Brother Lucius. The leech—whose head was entirely bald and bore a strange birthmark in the shape of an almond—smiled and nodded at the priest's story.

"Then I lunged for that bandit's dagger," Father Paul was saying, "but only got hold of his belt. 'Twas lucky for him; I am expert with a blade."

Brother Andrew had said Father Paul was a knight in the Crusades. He'd come back from war a changed man and devoted his life to God by becoming a monk. Yet, he often told tales of his knightly exploits—quite a contrast from most other monks, who barely spoke a word throughout the day.

"Coins flew everywhere," Father Paul continued. "And I grabbed a parchment from him—quite an important one, I think, with a wax seal and everything. Alas, then he kicked me and fled, the coward." The monk's story ended in a coughing fit.

"Good morning," Lucy said, walking into the room with the blanket. "This is for you."

Father Paul beamed with pleasure as Lucy and Maud spread out his new blanket over the bed, with the help of Brother Lucius.

The priest's story had been a bit exaggerated, of course, but it was essentially true. He had grabbed at a parchment that fell from Rummy's pouch, and the bandit had ripped most of it from his hands. But how did Father Paul know the document had a wax seal? This could be a clue.

"Father Paul," Xan said. "Do you still have the parchment from that bandit?"

The priest nodded. "Aye, a piece. Where did you put that cursed thing, Lucius?"

Brother Lucius stepped to a small desk and brought over a jagged piece of parchment, about the size of Father Paul's palm.

"May I look at it?" Xan asked.

The leech handed it to him. Sure enough, the edge of the page had been sealed in red wax—two swords, a serpent, and a cross.

He handed it to Lucy. "That's odd," he said. "I know this seal. 'Tis from Lord Godfrey. I saw it in Chadwick and again today in a book."

She examined it. "The bandit had this with him? Whatever does it mean?"

It meant that Rummy had gotten hold of an official document from Lord Godfrey's estate. Had he attacked Chadwick or waylaid some poor traveler who carried the document? Or perhaps he lived right under Lord Godfrey's nose. If someone had seen the bandit in Chadwick, with his jagged scar and swollen nose, they'd definitely remember him.

That might lead to another clue, and then another.

"I don't know what it means," he said. "But I aim to find out."

Roger

More rains came that evening—the fourth night since anyone had seen the Shadow. Of course, two of those nights had been rainy ones, and no one had ever claimed to see the shadowy figure in a rainstorm. That could be either because of the deep darkness of the storm or, more likely, because the Shadow truly was a monk who had no reason to walk outdoors in the pouring rain.

Friday morning brought a clear sky and a frigid breeze. In a month it would be winter.

Xan pulled a long-sleeved, woolen shirt over his tunic. It had been provided by the nuns yesterday, who had delivered to the abbey several bundles of clothes and linens: extra blankets for the night and brown, thick shirts for the day.

Brother Oscar made all the boys stand beside their beds, as usual, as he led them in the Lord's Prayer. Though Xan had not known the words of the prayer on the first few days of this ritual, he had memorized them by now, beginning with "Our Father, which art in Heaven."

While he prayed, he held the abbot's whittled cross in his palm. As he repeated the words, "deliver us from evil, amen," a familiar feeling settled upon him.

He'd stood and prayed like this before, in his prior life at Hardonbury.

There was no flash of light in his mind this time, no stunning vision, only the misty image of a man and woman on either side, holding his hands. Their faces became clearer: Mother and Father, lips moving in prayer. Mother had her eyes closed, her rosy cheeks still and peaceful.

His heart sank. He would never know what that felt like, praying with his family. He'd lost that chance forever now. But this new memory—if that's what this was—proved his parents had taught him to pray, though he might not be able to recall any specific prayers.

"Now, boys, take a moment of silence to offer your day to our Lord," Brother Oscar said.

Xan squeezed the little cross. *Help me remember them, Lord. Help me solve their mystery.*

When prayers had ended, the boys breakfasted in the refectory, where Brother Oscar assigned them chores. He told Xan, Morris, and several other boys to work with the lay brothers in the granges, helping with the harvest. He told Joshua to sweep the abbey church.

"Not again," poor Joshua said, real tears welling in his eyes.

"Don't worry," Xan said to the boy. "We can meet up later this afternoon and have races."

As Xan exited the wide hall, John passed by him, bumping him with a rude shoulder that caused him to fall against the doorpost.

"Watch where you're going, clumsy," John said, heading to clean the stables.

Xan just shook his head and traveled to the granges, where he spent the morning with the other harvesting boys. They lunched with the lay brothers at midday, sitting on the wheat-covered soil as they ate their bread and green-topped carrots before being released from their labors.

Yesterday, Brother Andrew had told Xan to find him in the scriptorium after his chores were completed. The monk intended to teach him lessons each day between the morning chores and *nones*, the monks' mid-afternoon prayers.

Xan found Brother Andrew and soon sat with him at the library table. But before his daily lesson began, he told the monk about Father Paul's parchment and Godfrey's wax seal.

"Indeed, that is strange," Brother Andrew agreed. "Perhaps you can ask Roger when he arrives. Maybe he has seen this Rummy at Chadwick."

"Sire Roger is coming here today?"

"Aye. We received a messenger early this morning who said to expect him ere *nones*."

What might be bringing Sire Roger here today, so soon after Xan's visit to Chadwick's sanctuary area on Monday?

The monk lifted Xan's school parchment up to the candlelight and reviewed the various sounds of the letter *g*. Over the next hour, he did the same for every letter and then wrote two letters next to each other, showing Xan how they could combine to make new sounds.

A bell rang in the abbey church.

"That must be Roger," Brother Andrew said, setting the parchment aside. "Come."

He led Xan to the chapter house again, where it seemed all the most important meetings took place at the abbey. Sure enough, when they knocked and entered, the prior and Brother Leo were sitting across from Sire Roger, sipping water from wooden cups and talking about the rains.

The edges of Roger's mustache had dipped into his cup so that water was dripping from it onto the nobleman's lap, while he squinted and wiped droplets from his deep-blue shirt.

"Ah, that poor peasant boy," Sire Roger said, when he glanced up and saw Xan.

Xan gave half a bow. "Good afternoon, sire."

"What is *he* doing here?" Brother Leo said, pointing at Xan.

"The boy has found another clue, Leo," Brother Andrew said, patting Xan's shoulder. "Go ahead and tell them, my son."

Xan explained about Father Paul's attack, scar-faced Rummy, and the wax-sealed parchment. As he spoke, Sire Roger's face went from interest to surprise to shock.

"I cannot imagine how such a document could have come into the hands of a bandit," Roger said. "Lord Godfrey and all of us on his high staff use that wax seal for official letters, contracts, and even proclamations. If this Rummy is the same bandit who attacked Hardonbury, as you say, then perhaps he found the parchment in the manor house ere he burnt it down."

That made sense. Lord Godfrey must have had regular contact with the lord of Hardonbury because, after the fire, he'd abandoned his claims on the manor and transferred it to Godfrey.

"Actually, this boy's news relates to the purpose of my visit," Sire Roger said, slicking back a strand of brown hair behind his left ear. "I come with a message from Lord Godfrey."

The prior looked to Brother Leo and Brother Andrew. "Shall we fetch the abbot?"

Sire Roger held up a hand. "Not necessary. Perhaps this is a message best heard by you, Prior, and then passed on to your dear abbot after some reflection."

Xan kept his eye on Roger, who seemed tense. Maybe this had to do with Penwood Manor. That would explain why he wouldn't want the abbot around, at least based on how the previous angry meeting at the chapter house had gone.

"My lord is concerned—indeed, quite worried—about the safety of your dear abbey and its two manors. He knows how vulnerable you all are to the whims of evil men, such as these bandits, and he seeks to extend a warm hand of friendship to you monks."

Brother Leo was nodding, but the prior's gray-bearded cheeks were like stone.

"And what would Lord Godfrey like to do for us?" Brother Andrew asked.

"He sends me to see about negotiating terms so that he can protect this abbey and its two manors—especially Penwood Manor."

Sire Roger paused to drink from his cup, his narrow eyes flitting between Brother Leo and the prior as he sipped. He seemed interested in how the two monks were interacting.

"We should find out more about this offer," Brother Leo said. "The danger here has—"

The prior glared at the monk. "For the love of Eve, we are aware of your opinions on this matter, Leo. But I think Lord Godfrey would expect us to recognize his claim on Penwood Manor as part of this negotiation. Is that not so, Sire Roger?"

Sire Roger placed his cup back on the wooden table and wiped his mustache. "That is so."

Perhaps the monks should consider negotiating, as Brother Leo suggested. These bandits were evil. If the abbot didn't find a way to protect the abbey's manors, Penwood could burn to the ground, and more peasants might die, like Mother and Father.

And more boys might be orphaned, like Xan.

"'Tis not my place to make such negotiations," the prior said. "And our abbot is unlikely to be interested in such a discussion, as you well know."

"Do not answer too hastily, Prior," Roger said. He gestured toward Brother Leo. "Talk about it with your wiser monks. Perhaps the abbot would listen if you all spoke with one voice."

The prior stood. "I will think on it, as you say. Now, I thank you for your visit, but the time for *nones* has arrived. Our Lord calls us to gather in the abbey church for our prayers."

"Oh my—give up Penwood Manor?" Lucy said. She and Maud sat on the edge of the fountain in the ring of bushes, next to Xan and

Joshua. "If Lord Godfrey cares about our safety as much as he says, he shouldn't force the abbot to do that."

"Yeah," Maud chimed in, bunching up her eyebrows. "That's not very nice."

The two girls had wandered up the convent path late in the afternoon, with a pair of older nuns eyeing them from a distance. The boys of the dorm had just finished a game of blindman's buff, where they'd taken turns blindfolding each other and making the "blind man" tag someone.

Thankfully, John was still off with David, searching for toads near the woodland stream.

"Sire Roger didn't know anything at all about Rummy," Xan said. "That probably means the bandits don't live in Chadwick. As bailiff, Roger knows everything that goes on at that manor."

Finding a link between Chadwick and the bandits had seemed a major clue yesterday, but now it felt like he wasn't a single step closer to learning why those bandits had killed his parents. If Rummy had stolen the parchment from Hardonbury's manor house—the most likely situation—then the parchment meant nothing at all as a clue.

Xan sighed. "Maybe I'm not supposed to solve this mystery, after all."

"But you're the smartest boy at the abbey," Joshua said. "That's why you're being taught."

Lucy smiled. "You're smart too, Joshua."

"So am I," said Maud.

The water in the fountain flowed peacefully around the striped fish.

"I like this place," Lucy said, turning her head westward. "It lifts up my soul."

Xan gazed in the same direction her eyes had focused. An autumn rainbow of red, yellow, and orange leaves dotted the woodland behind the granges.

"Do you think, if I asked God for the answer, that He'd give it to me?" he asked her.

Lucy seemed in tune with God and faith and prayer. He, on the other hand, had just started learning the right words and begun muttering to God under his breath now and again.

She giggled at him. "Of course He would." Then her lips pursed together seriously. "But, like Sister Regina always says, you might not get the answer you want, or when you want it."

A stone flew through the air and splashed in the water, soaking Xan's face.

"Look! 'Tis Sire Clumsy and his lady, the fair Frog Face!" John's voice rang from a bush.

"Give her a big kiss, Xan." That was David.

Lucy's cheeks turned red.

"Leave us alone!" yelled Maud at the same time that Joshua shouted, "Go away!"

John and David's snickering faded as they headed toward the boys' dorm.

Lucy smirked. "That John of yours is almost as bad as Silvia back at the convent."

Maud stood on the ledge with hands on her hips. "Yeah, she's always bossing everyone."

"Once, she almost scratched another girl's eyes out," Lucy said. "Sister Cecilia had to pull her off the poor girl, like she was a rabid dog."

"She does sound a lot like John," Xan said with a laugh.

"You haven't been fighting with him again, have you?" Lucy said.

He frowned. "When he goes right, I go left; if he looks one way, I look the other. And every time he walks by, he mumbles something—I don't know what."

"He wouldn't dare start a tussle with that Brother Oscar around," she said.

"Well, you see he's got David turned against me now, too."

"Ignore them."

Lucy might be right. But ignoring wouldn't work if John was going to throw stones and shove him into doors. Eventually they'd have to finish their fight.

The way he'd tripped John's feet the other day during that scuffle, it was as if he'd known exactly what to do. Maybe he'd been in a lot of fights while growing up in Hardonbury. And if that were the case, then his home might not have been all that different than here at the abbey.

"It doesn't matter," he said. "From now on, all my free time will be spent alone, studying words in the library and trying to figure out this mystery."

Lucy gazed at him. "You're not alone, Xan. You've got God. And I'll help you."

"Me too!" said Maud and Joshua at the same time.

Shadow

That night, after Brother Oscar doused the candles, Xan lay on his mattress, hands folded under a sliver of moonlight. He made the Sign of the Cross, just as the monks did before their prayers.

When will my memories come back, Lord? Must I wait a year to know what happened that day in Hardonbury, and to know what happened to my parents, and why? You can do anything—will You help me solve their mystery? Please help me understand why these bandits are after the abbot, and protect him. And Brother Andrew too. And the prior. And Lucy.

He closed his eyes, yawned, and snuggled under the warm blanket the nuns had sent.

Lucy had said God would answer his prayers, but not always when he wanted the answers. That kind of made sense. Maybe God made people wait for answers for His own reasons. If God knew everything, then maybe there were good and bad times to get answers. God would know when to give them. But what would an answer to prayer sound like? Hopefully not a creepy voice.

A familiar feeling settled upon him again, along with that mist in his mind. From it came Mother's hand, soft and gentle, with slender fingers. She touched his cheek and kissed his forehead. "Good night, my sweet boy," she said. "Good night, Mother," his own voice responded.

Was that a memory to keep, or just a dream he'd made up and would forget in the morning?

His warm blanket flew from his body, ripped away in one motion. Cold air rushed over his skin, leaving goosebumps wherever it touched.

"Wake up, Xan!" The harsh whisper was so loud it couldn't possibly count as a whisper.

Xan jolted to his feet, shivering.

Joshua stood there—hair sticking up on one side of his head—holding Xan's blanket.

"'Tis back! The Shadow!"

Xan pulled the long-sleeved shirt over his tunic as he followed Joshua to the other window, where John was watching, David by his side. The cold floor burned at his bare toes.

For a moment, it looked like John might pick another fight with him, even though Brother Oscar slept down the hall. Instead, John took a step back and gestured to the window. "If you're not too scared to look, clumsy."

David moved over so both Xan and Joshua could see.

"Where is it, Joshua?" Xan said.

"Same place as last time." Joshua pointed. "By the trees. See it?"

Xan didn't answer. In the dimness from a crescent moon, a dark, hooded figure almost glided through the mist, walking from the woodland trail toward the hedge.

The back of Xan's neck tingled. The shadowy figure was definitely holding something in its hand, though who could say what it was from this distance. It couldn't possibly have been the scythe blade of the angel of death. Wouldn't that be much more noticeable?

John laughed nastily, while several of the other boys crowded the floor behind them.

"Oh, Sire Clumsy, you are so, so smart," John said. Then the bully imitated Xan's voice, except he made Xan sound like a high-pitched girl: "Nay, John, there's no such thing as shadows. 'Tis just your imagination, John. Oh, my!'"

"Who's it coming for tonight?" asked Joshua. "Another priest, like Father Joseph?"

Several of the boys were talking over each other now. One child looked about to cry.

John jumped on David's mattress and addressed some of the younger boys, scrunched up in their beds. "The last time we saw it, who knows who it murdered at Chadwick Manor?"

Everything was happening so fast, with a swirl of emotions inside Xan's still-sleepy mind: confusion, anger, fear. John was going to make this the worst night ever for those poor boys.

"Nay," Xan blurted. "That guard died of a heart attack, John. 'Twas just a coincidence."

The chaos in the room suddenly crashed into complete silence.

"What guard?" John said, looking genuinely perplexed for a moment. Then his face lit up. "Are you saying you've known this whole time the Shadow took another soul that night?"

Oh, no!

Xan had never mentioned the dead guard to anyone, not even Lucy. He'd really made the worst of things now. He'd just given John all the evidence he needed to terrorize the dorm forever.

"So, John's right," Joshua said. "Whenever that Shadow shows up, it takes a soul."

Xan shook his head. "People die all the time for all different reasons. Just because there's someone walking out there doesn't mean any of us are in danger. 'Tis probably one of the monks."

Joshua didn't look convinced.

"So says the clumsy one without a memory," John said, sniggering. "You're so brave."

This was a disaster, and it was all Xan's fault.

There was only one way to fix this, but it was going to take the courage—or maybe the foolhardiness—to do the unthinkable. If he let that shadow-thing out there disappear again, as he'd done last time, John would make sure the younger boys would never sleep in peace.

Fine, then. It needed to be done, and he was the only one who could do it.

"Like I told you," Xan said, taking his shoes out from under his bed. "Probably a monk."

"What are you doing?" squeaked Joshua.

Xan slipped the shoes on his feet. "John dared me to go down the last time this silly Shadow showed up. Now I shall take that dare."

John stopped smiling. "You're dotie," he said. Was there a trace of concern in his voice?

"Nay, you spoke truly, John," he said softly. "I should have gone out last time."

For once, John was speechless.

Xan cracked open the door. Brother Oscar was nowhere in sight, but snores spilled out from his nearby cell. He slid past the monk's door and down the steps.

Outside, the mist was getting thicker. His breath rose like wispy fog in the faint moonlight. Even with his shoes on, his feet in the wet grass felt as if they'd been frozen in a block of ice.

This couldn't possibly turn out well. If the Shadow were one of the monks, he might get in trouble, perhaps even a paddling. If the Shadow were an intruder, he might get attacked. And if it were the angel of death—still a possibility—he might lose his life. After all, two times the Shadow had been seen, and both times someone had died.

All right, God, this may have been a bad idea. Can You help me out of this?

His heart was beating almost loud enough for him to hear it. Yet, in the library beneath that painting, Brother Andrew had told him not to fear death.

"Get your senses about you," he said aloud, forcing himself to move through the mist.

He took cover at the corner of the hedge—the last place he'd seen the Shadow. Even though the wind was cutting like icicles, sweat clung to the inside of his tunic.

Just then, a branch cracked. A figure moved from the other end of the hedge, but it was not creeping near the trail to Lord Godfrey's estate. It was heading up the hill toward the abbey!

This was the closest he'd ever been to the shadowy figure but, in all this mist, he could barely make out more detail than from the window. It was dressed in a robe of dark, woolen material, the same as the monks wore. Its cowl hung so low over its head that it was impossible to tell from this distance if there was even a face beneath the hood. The angel of death in his nightmare had reached with bony, skeletal hands. This figure didn't seem to have any hands at all, unless they were tucked inside its robe.

Yet an object was at its side, so it must have had a hand of some sort to grasp with. Its body was blocking the object, but it appeared to be long and narrow, round and thin—a staff or reed of some kind, like the one he had seen on Brother Leo's bed that day he'd first met the monk.

Xan's paralyzed legs wouldn't move to follow it. John was right: he must be a dotie fool to do this. What if this were that bandit, Rummy? The young boys might find his dead body crumpled in a heap on the meadow in the morning. Then they'd have nightmares for all their days.

Except if he went back without discovering the truth, they'd have nightmares anyway.

The hooded figure reached the top of the grassy hill—limping slightly, as though in pain—and headed into the granges.

There was no use debating anymore. Xan couldn't go back to the dorm now without completing his mission. A crowd of young boys probably were pressed around the window slits, watching his every move. They were counting on him.

He followed the shadowy figure from a distance.

"'Tis just a monk," he whispered. Of course it was. Then why did he feel compelled to convince himself of that fact with every step? John's stories for little boys had spooked him, too.

Yet the evidence was against John. The Shadow didn't even know it was being followed. And why would a robed angel walk around taking people's souls, anyhow? With so many people dying everywhere, the angel couldn't possibly expect to collect all their souls on time at that speed.

The Shadow left the granges and followed the cobblestone path that led around the abbey complex. No angel would follow a path like everyone else, but a monk or a bandit would. And what kind of angel would be limping in pain? That was just nonsense.

Xan followed it past the abbey church and chapter house. He arrived at the monk's dormitory just in time to see a remnant of the Shadow's robe pass inside the door.

Now what? He reached the door. If he opened it, he would alert the Shadow to his presence.

He ran to the nearby window that led into the small supply room next to the infirmary. He pulled himself up over the edge, squeezed through the opening, and dropped to the floor inside.

He tiptoed into the hallway. Moonlight barely penetrated the dorm through a far window.

The Shadow's footsteps receded down the hall, along with the swishing sound of its robe.

Xan glanced behind him. A watery trail of footprints glistened on the stone floor in the faint light. Just as his own miserable feet were soaked with the chill dew from the grass, so also the Shadow's feet had left wet marks. What would John say to that? Angels didn't leave footprints.

He followed the wet marks through a second hallway.

The sounds suddenly stopped ahead, around that next corner.

He paused to listen. His heart practically stopped beating. He tiptoed ahead and peeked around the corner. There was the Shadow, standing still in front of a cell door. Perhaps it had heard his steps behind it.

Without further delay, the Shadow opened the cell door and passed inside.

But which cell?

He counted the doors. Brother Leo had taken him through this very hallway and stopped to open a door—the same door the Shadow had just entered.

"That's Brother Leo's cell."

So, the Shadow was Brother Leo? But why had Brother Leo been walking about the abbey at this hour, all by himself? Maybe this was some strange habit of the old monk.

He crept to the door and listened, but the cell had become as silent as a tomb.

One fact was certain: he was not going to knock on the door and ask Brother Leo to explain himself. He'd be safer tapping an angel of death on the shoulder than disturbing the grumpy monk.

He headed back through the abbey complex, over the granges and meadow, and up the stairs of the boys' dormitory. As he entered the main room, one child yelped in terror.

"What took you so long?" snapped John.

Xan gathered the boys around him and told them what had happened, being sure to include all the evidence that would disprove John's spooky story about the angel of death.

"Then he went into Brother Leo's cell," he finished. "So, that's that, just like I said. The Shadow has been Brother Leo this whole time. No need to fear."

Several of the younger boys looked visibly relieved. Perhaps they would be able to sleep tonight, after all. But John was shaking his head.

"Brother Leo is dead." John stated it as certain fact. "The Shadow has taken his soul."

"Did you even hear a word I just said?" Xan asked. "That was no angel out there."

"But remember Father Joseph?" said John. "Remember the dead guard?"

"Remember Brother Leo's paddle?" Xan rolled his eyes. "Use your head."

Several boys laughed at his reference to John's public paddling.

John turned red and balled his hands into fists. Perhaps Xan shouldn't have humiliated him.

"Now, let's get back to bed," Xan said, stretching and yawning.

He returned to his mattress by a different route, making sure to avoid John, who looked ready to start a fight. He pulled his warm blanket over his body and bid everyone a good sleep.

The other boys, following his example, did the same. Even John lay back down.

Except no one had asked the one thought nagging at his mind. Why had Brother Leo been walking around the abbey grounds by himself in the dead of night?

Attack

Xan opened his eyes. The crescent moon had set; it was pitch black in the dorm.

Something had woken him up—a voice outside the door to their room. There it was again.

"By Adam, I have seen nothing amiss," said the trembling voice of Brother Oscar.

"We must check," answered another: the prior, Father Clement.

"As you wish, Father."

The door cracked open and the prior entered with a small lantern. The priest seemed to be counting the boys' heads in the dark, his finger pointing in the air. Then he departed.

"You are certain no one has intruded?" The prior was back outside the door now.

"No one, Clement. I hear everything from my cell. The children are safe, I assure you. But tell me: how has this happened to our poor abbot?"

What had happened? Surely this could have nothing to do with the Shadow.

"God only knows," the prior said. "Let me think on this further. I will make the announcement in the morning. Come. The abbot would not wish us to miss *nocturns.*"

Their footsteps faded away.

Xan pulled the warm blanket up to his neck. *What had happened?*

The monks had spoken about the abbot. Nay, he couldn't possibly be dead—not like Xan's parents. But what if he *had* died? John would say the Shadow took his soul, and then there would never be peace in the hearts of the orphan boys.

He whispered a prayer for the abbot and fell back into an uncomfortable sleep.

He stirred periodically through the night, but no voices returned. By the time he'd awakened the third time in the dark, he wondered if it had all been a bad dream. Then he remembered Mother kissing his forehead and touching his cheek, *"Good night, my sweet boy."*

After dawn, Brother Oscar woke the boys and led them in prayer, but the monk seemed distracted. Then he escorted them to the refectory. None of the boys mentioned voices in the night. Nor did they seem to notice the abbot's absence at his usual breakfast table.

As they ate their bread, John simmered, glaring in Xan's direction and shaking his head. Last night, Xan had not only proved John wrong about the Shadow, but he'd also made him look foolish in front of everyone. That had been a mistake. He'd probably want revenge now.

After the boys finished eating, Brother Oscar walked them over to the chapter house.

"We have a special meeting this morning," the monk said. "All the children are invited."

The chapter house already was filled with novice boys and convent girls, murmuring to one another with curiosity. This must be the time of the announcement the prior had mentioned.

"They've never done this before," David muttered as they filed into the crowded room.

The prior and Sister Regina stood up front, along with the novice master. The novices were huddled away from the orphaned boys, as though they didn't want to be associated with them.

Where were the other monks, like Brother Andrew and Brother Leo? And where was Lucy?

Xan scanned the room until he saw her. Their eyes met. In silent agreement, they wound among the others until they stood side by side.

"What's happened?" Lucy asked.

He stood closer to speak into her ear. Her hair smelled like sweet soap. "Last night—"

The prior cleared his throat, interrupting. "Please pay attention. I have an announcement."

A hush spread across the room.

"We ask for your prayers today, children," the prior said. "Something has happened."

Several of them murmured again. A few of the younger boys asked each other whether John had been right about Brother Leo's death at the hands of the Shadow.

"Quiet, please!" The prior waited for the children to be still again. "Regrettably, our abbot took seriously ill last evening. He is unconscious and in critical condition."

Thank God, the abbot was still alive. But why was the prior hiding the full truth from them? When the monk had come into the dorm last night, he'd counted the boys' heads to make sure none of them had disappeared. He wouldn't have done all that if the abbot simply was ill.

"'Til the abbot recovers, I will rule in his stead," the prior said. "And as my first command, I declare today to be a day of prayer. Your chores are suspended so you might pray with all your hearts for our abbot, who has dedicated his life to God and this abbey. We will say a special Mass for the abbot's healing later this morning, after *terce*."

Brother Leo entered the chapter house and approached the prior. He walked slowly, seemingly in pain every time his robe swished up against his back. He whispered something into the priest's ear that seemed to disturb him.

"That is all for now," the prior said, as he followed Brother Leo to the door.

The boys and girls lined up to leave.

Xan grasped Lucy's arm, so soft to the touch. "Can you meet me at the fountain in a few minutes?" he said. "There's something odd about all of this."

The abbot's "sickness," coming so soon after the attack by the bandits, might mean the two events were related. Indeed, was it possible that these two attacks—as well as the Shadow, the burning of Hardonbury, even the death of Xan's parents—might be connected?

With their chores suspended, they might have time to solve this mystery together.

Lucy nodded as the girls streamed from the room. "We'll be there."

While the boys marched over the granges back to the dorm, Joshua walked by Xan's side.

"Too bad the abbot's so sick," Joshua said.

"There's more to that story," Xan said. "C'mon. Follow me and I'll tell you all about it." His heart was beating fast again as he led Joshua over the meadow to the fountain. This felt like a vital moment—the time to discover the reason God had sent him to this abbey. This might be the clue he'd been looking for to understand why his parents had died.

"And where do *you* think you're going?" Two hands shoved Xan hard on his back, sending him reeling to the grass as Joshua yelled out in surprise.

Another light flashed in Xan's mind—a husky boy with crooked teeth standing over him while Xan's lip throbbed and bled. The boy in his memory had punched his mouth in front of one of the cottages at Hardonbury. He was staring down and laughing at Xan, dazed on the ground.

"Xan, get up!" Joshua pulled on his arm.

The light vanished, but a memory remained. Aye, he'd been in a fight at Hardonbury with a bigger boy. He'd tried to stop the boy from doing something bad—the boy had stolen something from one of the other children. Then the boy had punched Xan in the face, and he'd fallen and cried.

Xan got up in a daze. There stood John and David. "You didn't think I'd let you get away with that smart mouth of yours, did you?" John said.

Lucy and Maud rushed over to them from the fountain nearby. "Leave him alone!" Maud yelled, her little fists raised in the air, her long hair wild.

"Stop this right now," Lucy said.

"Stay out of this, Frog Face." John put up his fists. "This is about me and Sire Clumsy."

Xan shook off the strange memory that had stunned him. "Nay, I don't want to fight you."

John sneered. "Oh, but I want to fight you." He moved his hairy arms into a battle stance.

"John, we don't have time for this. I really need your help." Xan's voice almost had a pleading tone; anything to stop this fight. "Something bad is going on at this abbey."

David scratched at his curly head. "What are you talking about?"

"All of you, just listen for a minute," Xan said. "Then you'll see."

John held his fists high but stood back on one foot, giving Xan a moment to speak.

He told them about Carlo's search for the abbot, Brother Leo's disagreement with the abbot and the prior, the Shadow's walking into Brother Leo's room, and the voices speaking in the night about the abbot, concerned for the safety of the boys.

"Brother Leo should be dead," John said, lowering his fists. "Unless you're lying about the Shadow going into his room. It should have taken his soul."

"You can't be serious." Lucy put her hands on her hips. "A ghostly shadow who walks into monks' cells to take their souls? And I thought girls were silly."

"John, why won't you see that Brother Leo *is* the Shadow?" Xan said. "I don't know why he's always walking around out there. I don't know what any of it means. But we need as much help as possible to figure this out ere something else bad happens to this abbey."

"So, what is your plan, Xan?" Lucy said. "How can we help?"

Thank God that Lucy was here. Her focus and gentle demeanor were like the melody of a harp, singing peace and calm into an anxious moment.

"The way I see it, there are two things we need to find out," he said. "First, we need to know what *really* happened to the abbot last night. Second, I'm worried about Brother Leo and whether he might be involved in all this. Did you see how he came in and rushed the prior out of that meeting? We need to know what he's up to today."

"Sister Regina will know the truth about the abbot," Lucy said. "Maud and I can go talk to her. She's kind and quite clever. She'll tell us if we ask."

David looked to John. "I wouldn't mind finding out what that grumpy monk is up to. It would be nice to get him back for all the mean things he's done to us."

John smirked. "That sour old monk does have a lot of revenge coming to him, doesn't he?"

Thank you, God. The plan was coming together as if by a miracle.

Xan raised a hand to John in peace. "If you and David want to spy on Brother Leo, then me and Joshua can go find Brother Andrew. He's one of the obedientiaries appointed by the abbot, so he knows just about everything that goes on at this abbey. He'll know what to do."

They all looked to each other. They seemed to be in agreement.

"Fine, then," Lucy said. "Why not have all of us meet at the abbey church ere Mass?"

Xan nodded. "Perfect. We'll meet at the church when we hear the bells toll."

Accusations

Xan and Joshua never found Brother Andrew, no matter where they searched. He wasn't in the library, the chapter house, the scriptorium, or the church, where several monks hurried around the altar preparing for Mass. The other monks had prayed *terce* and departed a while earlier.

Then the abbey bells rang out, summoning all for Mass. Xan and Joshua waited for the others. Soon, Lucy and Maud hurried up the path, John and David close behind them.

When they'd all gathered to the side, Xan told them he'd failed to find Brother Andrew.

"We had better luck than you, then," Lucy said. "Sister Regina told us—"

"—that someone beat up the abbot in his bed," Maud interrupted.

"Hit him with a club or something, while he slept," Lucy finished.

David stepped closer. "And you were right about that Brother Leo. He's up to no good."

"Yeah, that stinky monk is definitely suspicious," John said. "We followed him into the forest, near those hedges where we've seen the Shadow. There's a little path behind there."

"But we couldn't follow too closely," David added. "He would have seen us."

John pointed back over the granges. "After a few minutes, the old grump headed back toward the abbey. But he had something stuck up one of the sleeves of his robe."

"A sword?" Joshua's eyes doubled in size, nearly touching the freckles on his cheeks.

John smirked. "Not likely. 'Twas thick and bumpy."

David lit up. "It could have been a little club, maybe."

"Whatever it was," John said, "he brought it back to the abbey somewhere."

"That's when the bells rang, and we came here," David said.

As they spoke, the abbey church filled with monks and servants, boys and girls. Brother Leo walked past, slower than usual. The last to arrive was Brother Andrew, followed by the prior.

"Brother!" Xan said, rushing to him. "Can we speak with you?"

"After Mass, my boy," the monk said, out of breath. "Come, get with the other children." There was nothing else they could do except obey and join the others within.

During the service, the prayers and readings passed over Xan's head like the wind. Why hadn't the abbot's attacker used a sword? It was as if he only wanted to injure the old monk, not kill him. And how did any of this reveal anything about the death of his parents?

Xan whispered a prayer for understanding as the monks chanted to God in Latin.

After Mass, the six children gathered out back to speak with Brother Andrew.

"I have but a moment, son," the monk said, looking stressed. "I must meet with the prior."

While the others listened, Xan told the monk all that they'd been doing, leaving out no detail. As Xan spoke, the light in Brother Andrew's blue eye seemed to dim.

"Such evil days," he said. "The prior and I have been in his cell fathoming who might have done this crime. Brother Lucius saw a robed figure leave the abbot's house last night with his cowl drawn over his face. We assumed 'twas an intruder disguised as a monk."

"Nay, it must have been Brother Leo," John said, perhaps a bit too brightly. "He's the attacker. Look at the clues." He listed each fact again. "See? They all lead back to Brother Leo."

"But he's a monk," Maud said.

Joshua nodded. "Yeah, a monk wouldn't hurt anyone, right Brother?"

The monk didn't answer. Maybe he was trying to find an answer other than the one John had suggested. Of course, he wouldn't want to accept that his friend had turned evil. But then, he'd said monks sometimes stray from the path of God because of the temptations of the world.

"You're right, Joshua," Lucy said. "Brother Leo wouldn't hurt a holy man like the abbot."

"But Brother Leo isn't like most monks," John said. "He probably hit the abbot with a club and then hid it in the woods. That must be when Xan followed him back to his cell."

"But why hurt the abbot?" Lucy asked. "It makes no sense."

"You heard Xan," John said. "Brother Leo's scared of those bandits. He wants Lord Godfrey to send guards down here to protect him, but the abbot won't allow it."

"Scared of bandits? Really?" Lucy sounded skeptical.

John's theory sounded a bit odd, but hadn't Xan been heading toward a similar conclusion? As manager of Penwood, Brother Leo had turned red when the abbot refused Godfrey's help.

"Enough!" Brother Andrew said, his tone sharp. "The rest of you get back to your rooms and pray. Xan, you come with me to speak with the prior."

He followed Brother Andrew down a cobblestone path, the monk marching two paces in front and mumbling to himself. Brother Andrew had never seemed this agitated before.

For a moment, in the mist of Xan's mind, he was walking two steps behind another man—Father. They were heading to a field with tools. Father turned and smiled, *"Come along now, son. Stay close."* Somehow, inside, he knew that was the day Father had taught him to thresh wheat.

Soon they came to the chapter house, where the prior sat at a table with Brother Lucius, the leech. As Brother Andrew entered, the prior stood. "Ah, you are finally here, Andrew. I sent a servant to fetch Leo, so we will begin our meeting shortly."

The prior noticed Xan and waved to him. "I see you brought this clever boy again, Andrew. Unfortunately, I do not believe it appropriate for children to attend this particular meeting."

"First hear what he has to say," Brother Andrew said, motioning for Xan to sit at the table.

Xan repeated all he'd said earlier, including the theory John had proposed that Brother Leo was the attacker. The monks were shaking their heads in disbelief by the time he'd finished.

"Jude's folly!" Brother Lucius said. "I would not make lightly such scandalous accusations against a man of Leo's good reputation."

"But I followed him over the granges," Xan replied. "He had his cowl over his head, just like the figure you saw." That one truth could not be denied, no matter how odd John's theory.

The prior put his hand to his graying beard and pulled his cheek. "That may be, child, but the idea that one of our own order would commit this evil against our abbot. Who can believe it?"

"The circumstances are strange," Brother Andrew said. "But these are troubled times for our abbey. Must we not look into this possibility, Clement?"

The prior made the Sign of the Cross. "Aye. We cannot allow a poisonous rumor such as this to work its evil in our community."

"And if it turns out to be true, shall we call the sheriff and bring criminal charges against one of our own?" Brother Lucius asked, scratching at the almond-shaped birthmark on his head.

"Criminal charges against whom?" Brother Leo marched slowly through the doorway. He glared at Xan. "I thought this was going to be a private meeting, Prior."

"The boy is here for a purpose." The prior pointed to a chair. "Please, sit down."

"Criminal charges against whom?" Brother Leo said again, folding his arms as he stood.

The prior sighed. "Something has come to our attention, Leo. As the temporary head of this abbey, I have no choice but to ask you a few questions. I pray you will speak the whole truth."

Brother Leo pointed at Xan. "I will say nothing in the presence of a child."

From the first day they'd met, the old monk hadn't seemed to like him. But it might not be a personal grudge. Maybe the monk just didn't like children at all.

"But you must," the prior replied. "This child has details that inform our questions. You deserve the chance to dispel all suspicions."

"What suspicions?" Brother Leo's crazy eyebrows stuck up worse than usual.

The prior cringed. "That, perhaps, you may be involved in the attack on our poor abbot."

He'd said the accusation as gently as any could, yet even Xan could feel the humiliation as it spread over the old monk's face. It felt sad to see it.

"By Peter's staff, have you lost your wits?" Brother Leo said.

The prior continued in a soft tone. "This boy saw you last night, walking about on the granges with your cowl over your head, just like the robed assassin Brother Lucius saw. Some wonder whether there is a connection 'twixt you and the abbot's injuries."

Somehow in all this, Xan had become the monk's accuser. All he'd wanted to do was solve his parents' mystery. How had matters gotten so out of control?

"This is an outrage!" Brother Leo cried. "Why would I attack my dear friend?"

The prior's voice remained steady. "Your disagreement with the abbot about Lord Godfrey is well known. Some wonder if you may have acted out of fear of those bandits."

"Fear of losing this mortal flesh?" Brother Leo's cheeks turned shiny and pink. "Saint Paul tells us to discipline this mortal body and make it our slave."

The monk had said something similar to John as he'd paddled him in the grass that day.

The prior threw up his hands. "Were you or were you not the one this boy saw last night, with your cowl drawn over your head? 'Tis a simple question—aye or nay?"

"Nay—I mean, aye—I mean, perhaps." Brother Leo's voice cracked. "I did walk awhile on the abbey grounds ere *nocturns*."

"Without permission?" The prior sounded skeptical as he picked at his beard.

Brother Leo's voice dropped to a whisper. "I *do* have permission. But only the abbot knows why I sometimes go to secluded places, away from all eyes and ears."

"I am your prior, yet I do not know about this arrangement. How strange that the only person who can verify your claim is unconscious and on the verge of Heaven."

"Then you must simply take my word as a man of God."

The prior glanced at Xan, as though he expected him to stand up and hurl more accusations at the angry old monk. Nay, he'd said too much already. Brother Leo had more than enough reason now to take the paddle to his backside even worse than he'd done to John.

"There is additional evidence, Leo," the prior said.

"Then out with it!"

"Today, you went into the woodland and brought back an item in the sleeve of your robe."

"And why does that matter?"

"I just ask a question, Leo. What did you hide in your sleeve?"

Brother Leo hesitated. "'Twas my prayer scroll. I forgot it in the woodland last night."

The other monks glanced at one another. Surely they weren't accepting that explanation.

"You took your prayer scroll into a dark forest with a chill breeze that would blow out any candle?" The prior shook his head in disbelief. "Does anyone else have a question for this monk?"

Brother Andrew raised a hand. "I wonder only one thing, Leo. Have you had any recent contact with Lord Godfrey or anyone from his manor?"

That was exactly the question Xan wanted to ask! Perhaps the key to this was in Chadwick.

"What are you implying? I have never in my life even visited Chadwick Manor." Brother Leo's eyes grew fiery as he stormed toward the door. "By Peter's staff, I will speak not another word to this devil's inquisition. If you think me guilty of a crime, Prior, then call for the sheriff."

The old monk exited and slammed the door behind him.

"What now?" Brother Lucius said, his bald head resting despairingly in both his hands.

The prior sat back, stroking his beard. "What would the abbot do if he were here?"

Brother Andrew put his hands on his hips. "The abbot would send me and the boy to Chadwick tomorrow to verify that Leo has not traveled there. If Leo is telling the truth about that fact, then I believe we must take him at his word as a man of God."

"But what is your theory?" the prior asked. "Why would Leo travel to Chadwick?"

"Leo now manages Penwood Manor," Brother Andrew said. "Remember how eager he was at that meeting with Sire Roger to find out the terms Godfrey wished to negotiate with us for protection. Perhaps he traveled to Chadwick to learn the details of those terms and has now decided to take matters into his own hands so that the abbot—or you—would be more likely to agree."

The prior nodded but then became angry. "If it turns out Leo is lying, I will throw him in the confinement cell myself. Indeed, Andrew, if he lies, you shall seek Godfrey's help in bringing a charge before the sheriff. That wicked monk can face justice in the King's courts."

The prior's anger might be mixing him up. Monks weren't supposed to like the King.

"I thought the abbot didn't want the King meddling in the abbey's business?" Xan said.

The prior paused. "You are right, but I will not see our own monks sitting in judgment upon one of their brothers who attacked his own abbot. It could tear this community apart."

Brother Lucius nodded. "And also the King's courts can do something our Church courts cannot: hang a wicked monk by the neck 'til dead."

There would be Brother Leo hanging from a royal executioner's noose. If that happened, would Xan be responsible for his death because he'd been the one to raise these accusations?

Investigation

O n Sunday, Xan and Brother Andrew left for Chadwick after
morning Mass. The prior had sent them on the journey,
despite it being a day of rest, because they needed to resolve
the issue quickly.

Xan had spent Saturday afternoon at the fountain with Lucy, Maud,
and Joshua.

"What will you do if Brother Leo is telling the truth?" Lucy
had asked.

He'd shrugged. "Guess we'll need to find another suspect then."

But in the dorm last night, John had been certain Brother Leo would
be proven a liar. "None of us is safe round here 'til that monk is thrown
in jail," John had said to the younger boys, in an eerie voice. "For all we
know, he might come in and kill us all tonight!"

Their journey to Chadwick was uneventful, with somber conversation about Brother Leo and the need to stay close to God to avoid the
temptations of the secular world. Mother and Father had been peasants with almost no worldly possessions. They must have been very
close to God.

When they finally arrived at Chadwick's manor house in midafternoon, Sire Roger received them with very little delay. He met them in the common room, where manor servants brought them water and bread, as well as a strip of meat and a honey wafer. Because it was Sunday—a day to celebrate the Lord's Resurrection—the rules even allowed Brother Andrew to eat some of the refreshments.

"Please come and sit," Sire Roger invited them, twirling the edges of his slick mustache. "You have traveled a long and weary journey."

After the customary pleasantries, Brother Andrew related the news of the attack on the abbot.

Sire Roger gaped in shock. "How can I aid your prior? My lord's offer still stands open to protect your abbey and its manors. There is the matter of Penwood, of course, but—"

"I apologize," the monk said, "but that is not the reason we have come. Indeed, the prior has made clear he will honor the abbot's wishes about Penwood as long as the abbot lives."

The problem always seemed to come back to Penwood Manor. Why couldn't that wealthy landlord just leave the poor abbey alone and allow it to run its two manors in peace?

"I see," said Sire Roger, his narrow eyes hidden in shadow. "Then why are you here?"

Brother Andrew looked to Xan sadly. "Tell him, my son."

"Aye, Brother." Xan cleared his throat and wiped his sweaty palms on his tunic. Perhaps the monk thought he was doing Xan an honor by letting him explain, or maybe Brother Andrew couldn't bear to say the words himself.

Xan explained the evidence against Brother Leo, slowly and with a trembling voice. Sire Roger groaned at the revelation the monk may have attacked the abbot in a misguided effort to get Godfrey's protection.

"We simply seek to verify some of Leo's statements," Brother Andrew added after Xan had finished. "If you do not mind."

Sire Roger hesitated. "I would hate to bring more trouble on your poor brother. He seemed to be a wise monk when I met him at the chapter house last week."

Of course, Sire Roger thought Brother Leo wise—he'd been the only monk to speak in favor of Godfrey taking control of Penwood. But Sire Roger might not have thought Brother Leo to be so wise if he'd taken the abbot's side against Godfrey.

"So you have not seen him, except at that meeting?" Brother Andrew asked.

Sire Roger turned his head away. "I wish that were so, Brother. Truth be told, I saw your Leo with Lord Godfrey the other day. As you say, he fears bandits and is eager for our protection."

"Pardon me, sire," Xan said. "Are you saying that Brother Leo recently traveled *here*? To this manor? He spoke with Lord Godfrey personally?"

If that were true, then Brother Leo had told a most treacherous lie last night. That would make it all the more likely that he was the robed assassin Brother Lucius had seen.

Sire Roger cast his glance to the floor. "I fear so. But, Brother, I would never think this Leo capable of murder. He seemed such a peaceable man of polite speech—not at all the type to harm a soul." The bailiff shook his head. "By my word, one cannot know the true evil in a man's heart."

Brother Andrew asked only one or two more questions. His sorrow seemed to rob him of all curiosity, like when Xan had learned from Old Tom about Mother and Father.

"Sire, thank you for your hospitality," the monk said, his eyes darkening with despair. "You have told us all we needed. There is now only one thing that must be done. Is your lord here today?"

Sire Roger's eyebrows raised in surprise. He shook his head. "Do you require something else? My lord has been traveling for a few days but will likely return tomorrow."

Xan's stomach turned. Events were speeding out of control, like the raging fire that had swallowed Hardonbury. The prior had already decreed that if Brother Leo were lying, he would be dealt with by the sheriff. That meant the King's courts and a meeting with the hangman.

Brother Andrew hesitated a moment. "Aye, there is something. The prior seeks the help of your manor in one matter. Is not Lord Godfrey kin with Walter of Elton, the sheriff?"

"Well—I mean—aye, they are cousins." Sire Roger twirled his mustache harder. "But surely your prior will not involve the sheriff and royal courts! With all the struggles 'twixt our King and your Pope, I assumed you would keep this case at your abbey in your own holy courts."

"Perhaps we will invoke the clerical privilege in the end," Brother Andrew said. "But for now, the prior wishes to pursue the idea of charges with the sheriff and the royal courts. He fears the scandal it might bring to our monks to have to sit in judgment on one of their own."

Sire Roger frowned. "I do hope the prior changes his mind. Yet, if you insist, I will arrange a meeting here at Chadwick 'twixt you and the sheriff."

Brother Andrew gave a gracious bow to the bailiff. "Thank you, sire. We will await your messenger with word of this meeting. And may God guide us all during these troubled times."

Xan also bowed before they departed down the path and into the woodland.

As they journeyed back to the abbey, Brother Andrew wiped a tear from his face. "Curses and evil days! Brother Leo lied. Did the fool not think we would investigate?"

"But could he truly be hanged by the King's courts?" Xan said. "Even Sire Roger was unhappy about that. If there are Church courts, shouldn't the abbey use those instead?"

Brother Leo surely was a bad monk, but killing him seemed far too harsh a penalty. Xan's parents had died, along with so many others. Why feed to Death yet another victim?

"You are right again, son," the monk said. "Indeed, I will ask the prior to invoke the clerical privilege, which allows the Church to stop monks and other clergy from facing justice in the royal courts. That, at least, is one holy tradition the King still respects."

They made it back to the abbey just after sunset and reported the day's events to the prior. The priest made a quick decision: Brother Leo must be placed in confinement that very night.

"What about the clerical privilege?" Xan asked, after the servants had left to arrest him.

Brother Andrew nodded. "Aye, Prior. The boy and I feel strongly about this. Do you really want to see Leo at the end of the hangman's noose? And what of the authority of our Pope?"

"I understand your concern," the prior said. "Yet a simple meeting with the sheriff will not hurt the Pope. The sheriff has great experience in violent cases such as this. We need his wisdom ere we take a road that can tear our community apart from within."

Brother Andrew nodded. "True. The devil would applaud such a scandalous spectacle."

The prior raised his eyes to Heaven. "Why must I make these foul choices, O Lord? When will the abbot wake from this sickly slumber?"

Xan could not fall asleep that night despite his fatigue, even while the others snored in their beds.

"Good night, my sweet boy." Yet even Mother's words did not bring him comfort tonight.

God supposedly had sent him to this abbey to solve the mystery of his parents' death and to discover where he fit in this new life. Instead, he'd become the accuser of a grumpy monk who'd attacked an old abbot out of fear. Nothing seemed to be working out as he'd thought.

The monks always prayed in times of uncertainty like this one. Yet their prayers had not stopped the evil in the world around them. So what was the point of their prayers?

Xan closed his eyes and made the Sign of the Cross. *Lord, please help me to understand.*

Restless minutes passed in the darkness without bringing any further clarity. A sliver of moon rose and shone through the slits in the window, creating a gentle blue glow around him.

Just then, a rustling, like cloth rubbing cloth, sounded in the room somewhere. Xan turned his head in the direction of the noise.

There in the corner stood a robed and hooded figure, silent and still.

He strained his eyes to see. "Brother Andrew, is that you?"

The figure didn't answer.

It couldn't be the Shadow—Brother Leo was locked away in a cell. Unless Xan had been wrong, and the Shadow had been someone else instead of the monk.

"Brother Oscar?" he said, barely able to speak.

No response.

The figure began a slow march between the boys' beds. It didn't seem concerned with the others, just him. None of its steps made a sound, as though it were gliding over the floor.

That's when he saw that its hands were not hands at all—they were bony, skeletal fingers.

Were the stories true, after all? Was this the angel of death coming to take his soul?

"Xan," it whispered, with a hoarse, slithering voice.

It drew nearer, reaching out its bony hand.

He was trapped! A cry for help got stuck in his throat even as the Shadow's hand moved toward his face. His heart raced as his doom approached.

What would Mother or Father or Brother Andrew do right now?

"*When our Lord died on the cross, he conquered death,*" Brother Andrew had said. The monk didn't fear death. Neither did Mother or Father—they'd welcomed Death.

As the bony hand drew near to his face, Xan didn't yell or pull back—he would not allow himself to retreat. He too must embrace Death, just as those he loved had done. He shut his eyes tight. His heartbeat slowed; peace flowed over him; he stopped panicking and counted the seconds until his fate was sealed. Soon it would be over.

1 . . . 2 . . . 3. Maybe having one's soul taken wouldn't hurt that much.

Nothing happened.

He opened his eyes. The Shadow still towered over him in silence. Could he find the courage to speak to it? "What—What do you want with me?"

The Shadow's hand moved again; its ivory palm shimmered in the moonlight.

"What is that?" Xan peered into the dimness.

The Shadow's palm held a ripped piece of parchment—the one Father Paul had taken, with Lord Godfrey's seal on it.

Xan opened his eyes in a startle. He was all alone, except for the sleeping boys.

Had he just experienced a strange dream, or had that been a message from God? He'd thought the parchment had been his first clue, but then he'd decided it meant nothing.

Perhaps he'd been wrong about that.

Greed

onday morning brought a return to the boys' traditions: morning prayer, breakfast, and the assignment of chores. Brother Oscar gave Xan several jobs to complete, ending with the task of piling stacks of firewood behind the dormitory.

Before starting his first chore, Xan rushed to the infirmary, where Father Paul was still recovering. Following that revelation in his dream last night, it was all he could do to keep from running off into the chill darkness to retrieve the parchment.

Brother Andrew had said the Lord could work through dreams. Maybe the dream had been an answer to Xan's prayer. Perhaps Death was simply the servant of God, after all.

He entered the infirmary, where the old priest was snoring away despite the daylight. No one else was around. The ripped parchment lay on the desk, where Brother Lucius had left it.

Xan scooped it up and put it into the leather pouch on his waist. He'd be sure to bring it back later, after showing it to Lucy and Brother Andrew. Maybe he shouldn't have discarded it as a clue so quickly before. It still might have a part to play in solving this mystery.

He returned to the dorm and spent the morning on chores, avoiding contact with Joshua, John, and any of the other boys. Then he stacked the firewood into several piles and—before Brother Oscar could assign him another task—hurried down the trail to see Lucy.

Sister Regina was walking around the convent when he arrived, coming from the garden.

"What brings you here this afternoon?" she said, pushing a stray hair back under her habit.

"I was wondering if I could speak with Lucy. She's been helping me solve this mystery, and I wanted to show her a clue."

The nun gave a quizzical look, then peered into the afternoon sky as if to guess the time. "I believe Lucy is still praying in our little chapel after the midday meal," she said.

"Still praying?"

The nun laughed, but not in a mocking way. "Aye. 'Tis not a crime, you know. Lucy spends more time in the chapel than most of the girls, and—"

Just then, Maud exited the main door of the convent, followed by Lucy, whose face lit up as soon as she saw him. "You must have got back late from Chadwick last night."

He nodded. "Aye, and—"

"Brother Leo's in jail!" Maud interrupted, scrunching her dark eyebrows together.

"I know," Xan said. That news had traveled fast.

He quickly told them what had happened in Chadwick and how he'd dreamed about Father Paul's parchment. He pulled it from his pouch and handed it to Lucy.

"I'd given up on it as a clue, but now I'm starting to wonder if I missed something."

Lucy turned the parchment over and back again, feeling the seal and putting it close to her face. "Did you figure out what these numbers are here?"

"What numbers?" He took the parchment back. Several tiny faded symbols were inscribed directly above the edge of the seal. He'd seen them before but hadn't recognized them as numbers.

"May I see?" asked Sister Regina.

He handed it to the nun, and she made a pleasant "hmm" sound. "'Tis a date. That is common on official documents to place the date next to the seal. Very common."

Except Brother Andrew had not yet taught Xan about reading dates on official documents. It suddenly seemed that being lettered was absolutely necessary for solving mysteries.

"How odd," the nun said. "This parchment is dated less than a fortnight ago."

"Less than two weeks?" he said. He'd been at the abbey for more than a fortnight now.

If the document were that recent, then it was created after his parents had died. And if that were true, then Rummy could not possibly have stolen it from the manor house at Hardonbury.

He repeated his thoughts aloud for everyone to hear.

"Then it really *is* a clue," Lucy said. "Where did that bandit get it?"

Several other innocent theories still existed for that, including the possibility that Rummy had stolen it from a traveler who had done recent business at Chadwick Manor.

"But what if that bandit had got this document from Chadwick itself?" Xan said. "What if someone there gave it to him?"

Lucy's face turned a shade paler, making her hair seem blacker than usual. "Then Lord Godfrey could be involved in all this evil. 'Tis *his* personal seal on the document."

"Maybe that's why Brother Leo was meeting with him," Xan said. "Maybe that's why he attacked the abbot." If true, then that grumpy old monk was a greater villain than he'd thought.

"A conspiracy," Sister Regina suggested. "We must tell the prior immediately."

They hastened to the abbey complex just in time to find the monks exiting the church after *nones*. The monks lumbered from the arched doorway as though the energy of life had been sapped from their hearts. They must still have been in shock from the events of the past week.

The prior and Brother Andrew were standing within the narthex of the church, near the entrance to the building. They were talking in whispers with serious tones.

"What are you all doing here together?" the prior asked, seeing the group arrive.

"Another clue," Sister Regina said. "You would do well to listen to all this boy has to say."

Xan recounted the entire chain of events, including the date on the parchment.

The prior showed great interest. "Let me see the document." Xan handed it to the prior, who examined it and then passed it on to Brother Andrew.

"Indeed, this is Godfrey's wax seal, and 'tis dated just one day ere the attack on our abbey," Brother Andrew said. "By Adam, if Lord Godfrey has been involved in this evil this entire time—even conspiring with those godless bandits—that would explain much."

True. A conspiracy between Lord Godfrey and the bandits would explain the attacks on Hardonbury, the abbey, and Penwood Manor. It could solve the mystery of Xan's parents' deaths and even explain why the bandits had spared the fields of Hardonbury when they'd burned the rest. And if Godfrey were running low on his finances, new manors would help with that problem too.

What if that document Rummy held was a contract promising gold coins if the bandits made those attacks? Hadn't one of the bandits mentioned a reward? A reward from whom? Lord Godfrey!

Another memory flashed in Xan's mind. He was six years old, and Mother and Father were working in the fields. A neighbor (what was his name—Hubert?) came to him with a fresh apple, red and juicy. He'd pointed to a nearby tree, where the wind had blown the man's hat right off the top of his head and into the branches.

"Climb up that tree, boy, and fetch me cap," Hubert had said, "and I'll reward you with this here apple." Then Hubert had boosted him into the tree, and he'd inched to the edge of a branch to rescue the man's hat. The reward of the apple had been well worth the scratches from the bark.

Apples motivated little boys. Gold coins could motivate bandits. But what could possibly motivate Brother Leo to betray the abbot and his abbey?

"Do you think Lord Godfrey conspired with Brother Leo too?" Xan asked.

The prior hesitated. "Perhaps. That at least would explain Leo's actions beyond the mere fear of bandits. Godfrey might have offered him a handsome reward to ensure Penwood was transferred to his control. As manager of Penwood, Leo would be the perfect person to corrupt."

"Aye. Greed has corrupted too many monks through the years," Brother Andrew said.

Lucy looked perplexed. "Even if Lord Godfrey were to give riches to Brother Leo, where would he ever spend them? He can't use his treasure at the abbey. Where would he go?"

The prior spoke harshly. "To Lincoln; to York; to London. There are many places a wicked brother could flee, shedding his robe and embracing the pleasures of the secular world."

Brother Andrew rubbed at his brown eye sadly. "It seems then that this nobleman may use his wealth to control both holy and evil men."

"But why would someone be so bad?" Maud asked.

"'Tis like Brother Andrew told me," Xan said. "Powerful men are never satisfied. They always want more." But others, like his parents, were the ones who paid the price for that greed.

As they spoke, that same rage Xan had felt before rose within him again. "That greedy Lord Godfrey. My parents and so many others died so he could get that manor. If anyone deserves to be hung to death, 'tis him." He clenched his fists.

Brother Andrew put an arm around his shoulder. "Easy, my son. Justice will come in its own time. For now, these are but theories, though they are strong ones. What say you, Prior?"

Father Clement picked lint from his robe where it bumped out from his belly. "I say that I wish we had known all these things sooner. Lord Godfrey's messenger arrived this afternoon inviting us to meet with the sheriff tomorrow. Indeed, Godfrey himself will attend the meeting."

How had Sire Roger planned the meeting so quickly? He must have done it all yesterday.

Brother Andrew folded his hands. "I had not yet heard that unfortunate news, Father."

"Wait," Xan said. "If we're right about all this, it seems like a terrible idea to go to Chadwick and speak with the sheriff. Isn't he Lord Godfrey's cousin?"

"That he is," Brother Andrew said.

"Cousin or not," the prior said, "the sheriff is the King's man. He is the only one in the shire with the power to confront Lord Godfrey."

"But will he do it?" Sister Regina said. "Will he arrest his own cousin if it comes to it?"

Brother Andrew grasped the rope tied around his habit and started to fray one of the ends. "By Peter's staff, this will prove to be a dangerous business."

"And that is not the worst of it," the prior said. "The messenger told us that Lord Godfrey insisted on one detail: that we bring forth our evidence before the sheriff at the meeting."

"Bring the evidence?" Lucy said. "That sounds risky, doesn't it?"

"The girl is right, Prior," said Brother Andrew. "Bringing the evidence means bringing the parchment and Brother Lucius and even the boy. We are putting them all in danger."

The prior nodded. "'Tis a leap of faith, indeed. But we must lay our fears before the throne of God and trust our Lord to protect us, as the abbot has taught."

Too bad the abbot had made that statement just days before being brutally attacked.

Sister Regina looked to the sky again. "Lucy, 'tis getting late in the day, and your weaving awaits you back at the convent. We must go now."

"Goodbye, Xan," Lucy said, with Maud waving at her side. "Be careful tomorrow!"

"Aye, please do," Sister Regina added. "But do not worry. As Saint Paul tells us, 'God works all things for the good of those who love Him.'"

That was a comforting thought. Except how much good had been "worked" for his parents? They'd given their lives just so Lord Godfrey could get more riches. And even a monk had become corrupted as part of that evil scheme. So where was the good?

"'Tis settled, then," said the prior. "We will depart in the morning promptly after *prime*."

Brother Andrew smirked. "Aye, and we will be like Daniel walking into the den of lions."

21

Confrontation

The next morning—even as the abbot remained unconscious in bed—Xan and the three monks journeyed to Godfrey's manor. Along the way, the prior reviewed the evidence with them in detail.

"I must speak clearly on this matter," the priest said. "There is no room for error."

As they traveled, neither the freshness of the brisk air nor the blueness of the sky could clear away the heaviness on their hearts. Indeed, any sorrow for Brother Leo that had been in Xan's heart yesterday had turned more and more to anger as he'd fully considered the monk's treachery.

"I spoke with Brother Leo last night," Brother Andrew said. "He still will not discuss the matter or even provide a reason why he was walking the abbey grounds that night. Neither does he admit wrongdoing, though. He told me that I was playing the role of Judas."

The more they spoke about Brother Leo and Lord Godfrey, the angrier Xan got. The memories of Mother and Father had grown stronger this past week. He could almost feel the love that he must have felt for them back in Hardonbury. But Lord Godfrey had taken all that away from him just so he might add a few more manors to his collection. And Brother Leo had helped.

"Still, I pity the man," Brother Lucius said. "He rots in jail while we walk in the sun."

"I don't feel bad for him anymore," Xan said without thinking. "He must have known what Lord Godfrey did to my parents, but he still conspired with him. Maybe he *does* deserve to hang."

The prior turned to him sternly. "And who are you to pass judgments of life and death, child? If you cannot create life, why should you be so eager to destroy it?"

The priest had never reprimanded him before. Still, wasn't Xan right about the monk? "But, Prior, he's wicked and grumpy and vile!" Xan said, his anger still rising.

"Nay," the prior said. "You owe that monk more than you know. You owe him your life."

Xan turned to Brother Andrew, whose eyes gave no support. "What does the prior mean?"

Brother Andrew sighed. "'Twas Brother Leo that saved you in the forest that morning, my son. He heard your cries, found your body, carried you to the infirmary. That long walk was difficult for him. When he arrived, his robe was torn and his knees bloodied from all his falls."

Xan stopped, astonished. "Why didn't anyone tell me this ere now?"

"We could not," the prior said. "Leo forbade us from speaking a word about it. He never desires credit for his good deeds. He cared for you those days as though you were his own boy."

"But . . ." Xan's voice trailed off. "But he's always so mean and cross with me."

"That is his way with everyone," the prior said, more gently this time. "I understand your anger, child, but you deserve to know the truth ere you pass judgment upon such a man."

While the group trudged along the trail, Xan walked in silence. How could a man like Brother Leo do so much evil and yet have also done so much good? Perhaps he should be pitied rather than hated. It all might be a matter of a person's attitude.

For instance, Sister Regina had said God works all things for good. Was there good to be seen in all that had happened? Brother Andrew might say that Xan's parents lived in God's glory now. And perhaps God had also brought good from their deaths by sending Xan to Harwood Abbey. Had he not been at the abbey, would any of these clues have been discovered?

Eventually they arrived at the gates of Lord Godfrey's manor house.

As before, the lord received the delegation with grace and charm. After the customary inquiries, he and Sire Roger escorted his guests into a large, comfortable sitting room. Taller than anyone in the gathering by at least a hand's length, Lord Godfrey sat behind a great oak desk in a vest of red, gold, and blue, similar to the one he'd worn last time. On his right sat Sire Roger.

Sitting to the lord's left was his cousin, Walter of Elton, the sheriff. Though he might have worldly authority, Walter did not appear to be the stronger of the two cousins. His long, thin mustache seemed frozen in ice; yet, his eyes flitted from one person to the next, as though he couldn't make up his mind as to which person they should finally rest upon. That didn't bode well for the hope that the sheriff could take on Lord Godfrey, should the evidence warrant an arrest.

After they all had introduced themselves and taken their seats, Lord Godfrey spoke again.

"Good prior, I humbly offer you the services of my manor to handle this very sensitive issue. As you requested, I have invited my coz, the sheriff, to consider whether charges should be brought against your sad monk."

"Thank you, lord. I am glad the sheriff can be here today as the king's representative." The prior paused and took a deep breath. "You speak truly about the charges against our monk, Leo. But, my lord,

I am afraid to say that we come with even greater woe: evidence against you."

"Against me?" Godfrey asked, grace slipping from his voice. His eyes searched from person to person, as if looking for some hint of humor. Sire Roger looked equally confused.

"Aye, my lord," the priest said. "This is no child's prank. We suspect a dreadful conspiracy 'twixt yourself and our fallen monk."

This was the moment it could all come apart. The prior had been brave in confronting the lord, but if this were a lion's den, then Godfrey was about to set the fierce animals to their meal.

Lord Godfrey rose in anger. "How dare you make such a charge! I am mortally offended!"

Xan's heart pounded. Surely he would have them all killed now, or perhaps throw them into Chadwick's dungeon forever.

The prior didn't back down. "Let the evidence speak for itself, lord."

Godfrey—apparently uncertain about how to proceed—turned to the sheriff, who gestured for him to sit. "Please, Coz, let the monk bring his evidence. These are just words."

The lord wiped sweat from his vast brow and took his seat again, but only with reluctance.

The prior cleared his throat. "'Tis with great pain that we make these charges, lord. We love Leo, though he has never been a man of delicate speech. And while he can be cantankerous and difficult, we now believe he acted against our abbot only due to a conspiracy with this manor."

Xan shifted uncomfortably in his seat. The prior's words had triggered the memory of another conversation. Sire Roger had talked about Brother Leo's speech, too. Except he'd called Brother Leo a "peaceable man of polite speech." What an odd way to describe the monk.

The prior gestured. "Stand, Brother Lucius, and tell the sheriff what you saw that night."

The monk did so, describing the robed assassin with the cowl who had attacked the abbot.

"And this boy"—the prior pointed at Xan—"followed a robed man with a cowl over his head into the monks' dormitory that same evening. And where did he go? Into Leo's room."

"But," the sheriff said, "a child's testimony is absolutely inadmissible in our royal courts."

How insulting. Did the sheriff think all children were liars? Lucy, for instance, had more honesty in one of her slender fingers than Lord Godfrey had in his whole colossal body.

"I know the rules of evidence, Sheriff," the prior said. "In fact, Leo has not denied being outside that night with his cowl over his head. I heard that admission from his own lips, so the boy's testimony would be unnecessary on that point."

"Very well," the sheriff said. "But can you tell me why this monk would attack his abbot?"

The prior nodded. "Leo manages Penwood Manor. We believe he sought to personally profit by transferring the manor to Lord Godfrey's ownership. As you know, there is a dispute about Penwood's legal status, and our dear abbot has been insistent that the manor should never fall into secular hands. Leo has been equally insistent that Lord Godfrey get hold of Penwood."

Lord Godfrey slammed his fist on the desk. "This proves nothing! That some overly ambitious priest should attack his abbot is tragic. Yet young men often do impulsive deeds. But even if this man sought my protection for Penwood Manor, what crime is there in that, Coz?"

Xan's stomach turned. Why was he doubting the prior's words? Lord Godfrey had spoken with passion, as though he believed in his innocence; but the prior had spoken with confidence.

If Brother Leo had conspired with Lord Godfrey, then the nobleman must have known the monk enough to trust him. They'd probably met together and spoken at length about their plans. But Lord Godfrey had just called Brother Leo young and had even referred to him as a priest.

"There is more," the prior said, pulling the parchment from a pouch. "We have evidence connecting this manor with the bandits who attacked Penwood and then set fire to our abbey."

Lord Godfrey's eyes lit up in shock. He stood as if to interrupt, but the prior kept talking.

"Father Paul—too ill to be here today—ripped this from the hands of one of those bandits the night of their attack." He pointed at the parchment. "Look! 'Tis sealed with the wax of this manor and dated the night before those bandits struck. Examine it, Sheriff, and you will see."

He handed it to the sheriff, who studied it before passing it to Lord Godfrey and Sire Roger.

"This parchment," the prior said, "links Chadwick Manor to the bandits who attacked Penwood and our abbey. Indeed, if you would hear the testimony of this boy, he would tell you that one of the same bandits who attacked the abbey had also set fire to his poor manor at Hardonbury. The Scriptures tell us that through the mouths of babes the truth shall be revealed."

The prior pointed proudly toward Xan, who bowed his head in embarrassment and whispered a prayer under his breath: *Please help me see what I'm missing, God.*

The prior was right: the seal on the parchment definitely connected Rummy to Chadwick Manor. And Rummy was the same bandit who'd burnt Hardonbury. That much was certain. Sire Roger's report of the meeting between Brother Leo and Lord Godfrey had connected the monk to this manor, too, but Brother Leo had insisted that he'd never even been to Chadwick.

Xan himself had seen the evidence linking Brother Leo to the abbot's attack. The robed assassin that Brother Lucius described coming from the abbot's house was dressed just as the man Xan had seen walk into Brother Leo's room. He'd seen the Shadow just before he'd gone back to the boys' dorm, gotten into bed, and fallen fast asleep, only to be awakened by voices later.

Wait! That was the problem, wasn't it? That's what had been bothering him.

The prior had continued with his speech, explaining that Lord Godfrey had orchestrated all these attacks to expand the size of his estate. "This nobleman hoped that attacking with bandits would lead us to seek his protection and force us to settle the matter over Penwood. When that did not work, he conspired with Leo to harm our abbot and intimidate us into submission."

At each new accusation, Godfrey turned redder and his eyes burned with a raging fire.

"And," the prior said, "I have not yet come to the most damning proof, Sheriff. This final piece of evidence will prove the connection 'twixt your cousin and my monk from the mouth of one of his most trusted advisors."

Lord Godfrey rose angrily. He had lost all appearance of nobility and now twitched as fury pounded through his veins. "I have heard enough!" he shouted. "This is an outrage!"

The powerful landlord stormed from behind his desk toward the prior.

Sire Roger also sprang up, running toward the door, perhaps to get a guard.

The prior stood his ground, bracing for a blow from the nobleman.

Xan leapt to his feet. "Wait!" he cried. "I know what *really* happened."

22

Revelation

Something in the tone of Xan's voice caused Lord Godfrey to halt his approach.

"What is it, child?" the prior said, his confident eyes shaken.

A long silence hung between them before Xan spoke again. His heart beat faster than even when he'd followed the Shadow across the granges. Unlike then, lives truly were at stake now.

"Prior, we are mistaken," he said. "Lord Godfrey is innocent."

The prior gasped. "What are you saying, boy? Is this some prank that you—?"

"Silence!" the sheriff ordered. "Let the boy speak."

The prior flopped into his chair in humiliation.

Xan's voice cracked when the words left his lips again. "Lord Godfrey is innocent. He doesn't even know Brother Leo."

The nobleman bobbed his grand forehead up and down. "'Tis true. Very true."

"How could you possibly know that, child?" asked the sheriff.

"A few minutes ago," Xan said. "Lord Godfrey referred to Brother Leo as a 'young priest.' But Brother Leo is really old. And he turned down the chance to become a priest three times."

The prior stood. "Godfrey could be deceiving us, Xan—pretending not to know him."

The sheriff glared at the priest, who sank back into his seat.

"So, you believe this monk acted alone in his attack?" the sheriff asked.

"Nay." Xan hesitated. The poor prior would truly be shocked by his next words. "The truth is that Brother Leo also is innocent of these charges."

The prior gawked in disbelief. "Both of them innocent? But you saw Brother Leo the night the abbot was attacked."

"I saw Brother Leo," Xan said, "but I did *not* see the man who attacked the abbot. The timing is all wrong. I went to bed after I saw Brother Leo go into his cell. The attack on the abbot came hours later—I woke when I heard voices. You had come to check on the boys, remember?"

"Of course," the prior said. "Xan is correct. As soon as Brother Lucius saw the assassin, some of us rushed to the dormitory and convent to make sure the children were safe."

"But maybe this Brother Leo went back out after you followed him to his cell," the sheriff said. "What makes you so certain he stayed in his cell all night?"

"When I saw Brother Leo crossing the granges, he was moving slowly and limping, as though he were in pain. If he'd attacked the abbot, it would have needed to be earlier in the night, otherwise he never could have run away as quickly as Brother Lucius described."

Brother Lucius raised his hand. "'Tis true! That assassin was fast on his feet."

"So, 'twas not Brother Leo, praise God!" Brother Andrew said.

The prior pressed both hands against his face in distress. "Lord have mercy! I have thrown an innocent monk into jail. Tell us, boy, who did it then? Who attacked our abbot?"

Xan shrugged. "Probably one of those bandits disguised as a monk. I heard their leader—the one named Carlo—say they'd come to target the abbot during that first attack, when they couldn't find him. He must have come back to finish the job and get the reward that he mentioned."

The prior stood again. "Reward from whom? There might not have been a conspiracy with Brother Leo, but surely Lord Godfrey paid those bandits to kill our abbot."

Before the nobleman could take offense, Xan shook his head. "Nay, not him, prior."

"But why not? Then who is guilty?"

Xan smiled. The evidence had come together in his mind just as Lord Godfrey had risen from his seat and rushed toward the prior. It had all made sense once he'd thought it through.

Lord Godfrey clearly didn't know Brother Leo, so he'd never had a meeting with Brother Leo in Chadwick, as Sire Roger had claimed. There was no conspiracy between those two.

Perhaps Brother Leo had conspired with someone else—maybe Sire Roger. But nay, Roger had talked about Leo as a man of "polite speech." No one had ever described the monk that way because it was entirely untrue. That could only mean that Roger didn't know Brother Leo either.

So then why had Roger lied about the monk visiting Chadwick Manor?

Xan pointed toward the chairs where Lord Godfrey had been sitting. "'Twas Sire Roger—your bailiff."

"Roger?" said the sheriff, turning to the empty seat where the bailiff had been sitting. "Where has he gone?"

Xan scanned the room. The last time he'd seen Sire Roger, he'd been running for the door.

"He's escaped!" Xan said.

Lord Godfrey seemed less certain. "Nay, he has probably gone to get the guards. How dare you accuse him of this crime. I demand evidence."

Brother Andrew jumped to his feet. "I understand now! You will hear evidence from your bailiff's own lips, Lord Godfrey. His words shall return to condemn him."

Xan smiled at the monk. Brother Andrew had put the same pieces together and reached the same conclusion. "Aye. Sire Roger tricked me and Brother Andrew when we came to Chadwick on Sunday to see you."

"Sunday?" said Lord Godfrey. "Roger never mentioned you were here on Sunday. I was in my study all afternoon; I would have met with you."

"That's when he tricked us. He made us think Brother Leo had come to Chadwick and met with you. That's what made us think Brother Leo had been lying to us."

"Roger said that?" Lord Godfrey said. "I never even heard Leo's name ere this very day."

"But your bailiff was too clever for his own good," Brother Andrew said. "Roger did not foresee the abbey seeking to charge Leo in the royal courts. He simply assumed we would punish Leo at the abbey and that no one would ever uncover his lie to us."

"Once we asked for the sheriff," Xan said, "Sire Roger must have worried the truth would eventually come out. I think that's why he's run off just now, lord."

The prior bowed low to Lord Godfrey. "My lord, I owe you the deepest apology. I have accused you falsely and brought shame upon my abbey. Can you ever forgive me?"

But the nobleman ignored the priest's words. "Walter, ring the bell!"

The sheriff grabbed a golden bell on the desk and rang it. Guards entered from two doors.

"Where's my bailiff?" Lord Godfrey shouted in a booming voice.

"He has left out the back gate, my lord," a guard said. "Carrying a rather large chest, too."

"After him!" the sheriff bellowed.

Guards scrambled for the exits. The back gate led to a horse stable. Roger had brought Xan and Brother Andrew that way last week on the way to the Hardonbury sanctuary area.

Xan sprinted to the back gate behind several guards in thick uniforms with heavy weapons. He easily passed them by in his leather shoes, wearing only a tunic and a pouch.

"Come back, Xan!" Brother Andrew shouted.

Nay, he would not stop the chase. There was no way he'd ever let that murderer escape, especially not with a chest filled with treasure. Sire Roger was the one responsible for the death of Mother and Father. He was the one behind the attack on the abbey and Penwood and the abbot.

As he ran, other memories flowed into his mind: running with his friends in the East Meadow of Hardonbury; running with the sheepdog along the paths; running with Mother in the cottage having a tickle fight; running with Father to see the sunrise on the hill.

He ran faster, pacing along the cobblestones.

To his delight, there was Sire Roger, just up ahead. Every peasant the bailiff had met had stopped to greet him with a bow. That and the heavy chest had slowed him down significantly.

That villain would never make it to his horse now.

"Stop, you murderer!" Xan shouted.

Sire Roger turned and saw him and dropped the chest to the floor. It tipped over, spilling coins and jewels on the path. The man stooped and picked up a leather pouch—probably stuffed with more treasure—and ran down the path that led to the Hardonbury villagers and the woodland.

Xan reached the sanctuary area seconds after Roger had entered it, climbing a low fence.

"Stop that man!" Xan hollered. "He's a thief!"

A few of the Hardonbury villagers recognized Xan's voice. They pounced on Sire Roger, knocking him to the ground. He kicked and screamed and cried, "Get off me, you stinky filth!"

When Xan came to the spot where Sire Roger lay pinned to the grass, the old woman they'd met last week marched over. She gave Xan a wave: "Good to see you again, Stephen."

Then she bent down and gave Sire Roger a big sloppy kiss on his cheek. "That one's for you, me grace," she said, as he sputtered with revulsion.

Xan laughed, staring down at him, as Sire Roger glared back, helpless and pathetic.

"Smile while you can, boy," the bailiff said, covering his nose from the smell. "You will cry again soon when your abbey is nothing but a fiery wasteland."

Then the man gave a nasty cackle and threw up in the grass.

Battle

"B ring that treacherous worm, Roger, to the sitting room with us," Lord Godfrey commanded.

Xan had followed Sire Roger back to the manor house—two guards grasping the bailiff's arms and dragging him along as he whined and complained while the peasants gawked at him.

"Xan, you are safe!" Brother Andrew rushed to embrace him.

"The abbey may be in danger, Brother!" Xan said, recounting Sire Roger's threat.

He might not have all his memories yet—only a few had streamed to his mind, in fragments with no context—but one thing was certain: Harwood Abbey must not be harmed again.

Lord Godfrey towered over his bailiff, who dared not even raise his eyes to meet his lord.

"Tell us what you have done, Roger," the nobleman said. "We have known each other since we were children. I trusted you with my very life. Why have you done this?"

Sire Roger said nothing, his slit eyes focused on the floor, his mustache frayed and filthy.

"I'll bet he's been stealing from you this whole time," Xan said, drawing nearer. That feeling in Xan's heart must have been hatred, pure and undivided. He should punch that murderous bailiff in the face for his crimes. He clenched his fists but held them back. "Lord," he said. "Didn't you say your manors were running low on resources?"

Godfrey nodded. "I thought it quite unusual." He pulled out a dagger and placed it near Sire Roger's lips. "Tell the truth now, Roger—every bit of it—and I might spare your tongue."

The bailiff burst into tears, confessing between heaving moans that he'd been spending more than his share of the profits for years; that he'd nearly bankrupted the estate and needed new manors to refill its coffers; that he'd hired bandits to force local manors into joining the estate.

"Curses and evil days," the prior said. "This man will stop at nothing to satisfy his greed."

"What about the abbey?" Xan said. Lord Godfrey's dagger was close enough to reach. He could grab it from the lord's hand and stab this filthy killer in the heart as he deserved.

"What time is it?" Roger muttered, his face so drawn with fatigue that he looked sickly.

"Why? What have you done, you villain?" the sheriff said, standing next to his cousin.

The bailiff broke down again, spitting out phrases between sobs: "Stubborn old abbot—refused to compromise—the abbey—bandits—burn it all—to the ground—Penwood and Oakwood would be ours—today—at sunset."

Lord Godfrey rang the golden bell again and several guards appeared. "Gather the guards and saddle the horses! We ride this very hour!" he ordered. The men scrambled toward the stables to ready the journey.

Godfrey told the prior not to fear—that he soon would ride with three dozen guards, armed with bows and swords, to the defense of

Harwood Abbey. "As soon as the preparations are complete, we will take to the road," he said.

Sire Roger shook his head with genuine sorrow. "You will not make it in time, my lord."

"Jude's folly!" Brother Andrew slapped his robe and turned to Godfrey. "My lord, I need a fast steed immediately. Someone must get to the abbey and warn them ere 'tis too late!"

Lord Godfrey turned to a servant. "Bring Meadow out front to the monk this instant. Brother, he is our swiftest mount."

The monk took Xan's arm. "Come with me, my son. Prior, we will see you at the abbey."

"Godspeed, Andrew," the prior said, waving a hand of blessing over them. Then he turned to Xan and nodded. "A remarkable boy, just as the abbot said."

Brother Lucius made the Sign of the Cross and bid them good fortune.

Xan and Brother Andrew followed a servant around the side of the manor house, where guards in shirts of chain mail were already saddling their burly horses, brown and white.

In the center stood a white horse so noble and tall that it must have been Lord Godfrey's mount. Servants around it carried an enormous shield and an oversized sword, likely meant for Lord Godfrey to take into battle.

The servant led them to a high, brown horse with a white stripe on its muzzle. "This is Meadow," the servant said. "He is kind and gentle, but fast as the wind."

With a hop, Brother Andrew slid into the saddle as though he were an accomplished rider. The servant lifted Xan upon the horse's back, directly behind the monk. He clung to the monk's black robe and peered down at the dirt and rocks. A fall from Meadow easily could break his neck.

"Brother, do you know how to ride one of these?"

The monk chuckled. "Indeed, son. I was raised by my family to be a knight."

Brother Andrew a knight? The notion seemed unthinkable. He was a monk, worried about making all his prayers on time and copying the Scriptures in the scriptorium. Who had taught him to ride horses? Could he wield a sword, too? They might need one before days' end.

"Trust God, Xan," the monk said, kicking the horse's side. "He will have the victory yet." Then they were off at a speed so sudden and swift that it would have pulled Xan from the horse and hurled him to the ground if he hadn't clung so tightly to the monk's robe.

The noise of the galloping hooves echoed too loudly for Xan to speak to Brother Andrew on the journey. Nor could Meadow possibly run at this pace the entire way to the abbey. Surely the poor animal would need a rest at some point.

Yet onward the horse ran, with the monk murmuring prayers or chanting as he rode.

Xan just held on tight and thought about all that had happened. All his misery had been Sire Roger's fault in the end, with the help of evil men who now threatened the abbey once and for all. They'd taken from him the ones he'd loved so dearly.

He closed his eyes. There were Mother and Father. Their faces seemed clearer now, less clouded in a haze. Mother was beautiful, especially when she smiled. She had such a warm laugh, too. And Father, who had laughed much less, looked young—much too young to die.

A tear welled up in Xan's eye.

But then other people's faces appeared: Brother Andrew, Lucy, Sister Regina. Had they not become like another family? Though his old life had been torn apart, not all had been for loss. Yet, all might be lost today unless Brother Andrew and he could do something.

They couldn't possibly stop those bandits by themselves. But if God could do anything, dare he ask God to spare the abbey any more harm? Would God answer that prayer?

"The abbey!" Brother Andrew cried, pointing as Meadow galloped down the final stretch of the trail. The sun had not yet set, though that time was fast approaching.

Please, God, won't you answer this one prayer and save these people? Save my new family.

Harwood Abbey rose before them as the horse cleared the woodland and made for the meadow. From the looks of it, they had made it back before the bandits' attack.

They passed the hedges and halted Meadow at the top of the hill near the boys' dormitory. The poor horse was sweating and panting. Brother Andrew dismounted and lifted Xan down to the dirt.

"Good boy, Meadow," the monk said, rubbing the white stripe on its muzzle. "You did it."

Xan had been riding behind the monk for so long that he could barely close his thighs and walk. He stumbled at his first steps, nearly falling to the grass.

"Careful, my son. Get your legs back under you now. We will need you healthy."

Xan walked in a circle and stretched his arms and legs. "All right, Brother. I'm ready."

The monk gestured down the hill to the boys' dorm and then to the convent.

"Your job is to run like never before, Xan, and warn the boys and girls that the bandits are coming." He pointed away to the east. "See that little trail back there? Tell Brother Oscar and Sister Regina to take the children in retreat up that trail. They will find a cave that we monks used for storage years ago. They can hide in there 'til we come to get them when 'tis safe again."

"What will you be doing, Brother?"

"Alerting the monks and novices. We will evacuate the buildings and retreat up that hill to the south. There in a clearing lies an abandoned cottage, older than the abbey. We will be safe."

"But can't we stop the bandits from burning down the abbey? We'll lose everything!"

The monk smiled. "Nay, Xan. We will lose nothing. Everything of value will be safe. Our Lord will help us rebuild. He will bring good from this, you will see."

Brother Andrew once had said that all the things of this world—buildings and books and beds and paintings—were temporary and passing, one day to be replaced by the greater glory of Heaven. With that kind of faith, no wonder the monk seemed at peace even in the face of this evil.

"Now run, son! Run like your life depends on it, for it might. See, the sun is setting!"

Xan reached around the black robe to squeeze Brother Andrew in an awkward hug. "Thank you, Brother. Thank you for everything."

Then he ran down the hill as the monk mounted Meadow and headed toward the abbey.

Some of the boys were gathered on the grass near the dorm. When Joshua saw Xan running, he raced over with a joyous shout: "C'mon, Xan! You can play barres with us."

There would be no playing. Xan told the boys what had happened and found Brother Oscar on the steps inside. Though old, the monk could move as quickly as any novice when needed.

"I'm heading to the convent," Xan said, as he ran off again. "We'll meet you in the cave."

He hurried down the path faster than before, passing several girls playing by a stone wall and ordering them to follow him. As he drew near, shouting, several nuns rushed out the door, including Sister Regina. They accepted his direction and quickly gathered the girls for the retreat.

"Where's Lucy?" Xan said, looking around.

Sister Regina squeezed at her hands anxiously. "I sent her and Maud to deliver fresh washcloths to Father Paul. She should be back soon, but how will she know where we have gone?"

"Don't worry, Sister," Xan said. "I'll run and find them. You head to the cave." Before she could disagree with him, he was off again along the path. He ran directly past Brother Oscar, who was leading a line of boys toward the convent. The monk shouted something to him, as did Joshua, but he didn't pause to find out what they'd said.

At the top of the hill, he looked down at the main abbey complex. It was already abandoned. Monks and novices, all in a line, were crossing the field toward the south hill.

What about Brother Leo—had they released him from confinement? And were Lucy and Maud in that line too, or had they missed Brother Andrew's alert? He had to find out. He sprang into the granges and headed toward the abbey.

"Lucy!" he called, when he got to the cobblestone path.

There was no reply, except for the distant sound of thunder. That must be the bandits already—the last rays of sunlight had just slipped below the horizon.

He had no choice. He at least must check the infirmary to be sure Father Paul and the two girls had made it out safely. As the hooves drew nearer, he bolted through the infirmary door.

Empty! Then they had probably made it out safely, thank the Lord.

Foul voices hooted and screamed outside.

Where had he heard that before? Of course, he'd heard it at the abbey the night of the attack, but hadn't the bandits done the same thing at Hardonbury? Aye, he remembered now—Father running out of the cottage, leaving him with Mother.

"Check in there!" one of the bandits yelled outside the window.

"I will take care of this myself." That voice: it was Rummy!

If that bandit saw Xan, he'd be murdered no doubt. Rummy would finish what he'd started.

Suddenly a crash—perhaps the door being kicked—followed by booted steps in the hall.

"No one is in here, Carlo!" Rummy yelled. "They must have known we were coming."

Outside, the darkening twilight was broken with the sounds of smashing wood and hooves upon cobblestone, and shouts of anger and surprise.

Rummy's steps approached down the hallway. In a moment, the bandit would see him. Xan pulled himself up and squeezed through the narrow window that led outside. He plopped to the ground hard with a grunt and jumped back to his feet.

There stood Carlo on the path ahead, dressed in chain mail with a torch in one hand and an iron sword in the other. The bandit's eyes went wide with surprise as soon as Xan sprang up.

"You are that boy," Carlo said. "I would run fast, child, if I were you. There is someone inside there who would kill to see you again."

Xan stooped down and picked up a stone from the path. Aye, he remembered now. He'd thrown a stone at Rummy back at Hardonbury. He'd knocked him from his horse into the mud.

Carlo shook his head. The eyes of the green-eyed dragon on the thin rope around his neck shimmered in the torchlight. "If you throw that stone, boy, it shall be the last thing you ever do."

The bandit's words brought only hatred and rage to Xan's heart. This might be the very bandit who had killed Father. He once had thought Rummy must be the one, but now that some memories had returned, he knew better. Rummy had chased him far into the woodland before catching him near the abbey—near enough for Brother Leo to hear screams and find him on the trail. Surely some other bandit had already killed Father by then. Maybe this one.

"Where is the abbot?" Carlo said. "Tell me and you shall live."

Carlo would find the abbot. He would kill him, along with any other monk in his way—just to collect a reward. The lives of all those holy men were worth but a few gold coins to him.

The rage shot from Xan's heart to his hands. He flicked the stone at Carlo's head as hard as he could throw it, just as he'd done when he'd struck Rummy from his mount.

In an instant, Carlo dropped the torch and easily caught the stone in his hand. "Why would you do that, stupid boy? You could have saved your life, but now you leave me no choice but—"

The bandit stopped at the thunderous sound of hooves descending upon them. The light in his eyes flared with recognition. He spun around and held his sword high.

"*God wills it!*" A sharp, clear voice had shouted out those words as some kind of battle cry, followed by a chorus of echoes in repetition shouting, "*God wills it! God wills it! God wills it!*"

A bandit ran down the path. "Soldiers, Carlo! They shout the war cry of the crusaders!"

"Sound the retreat," Carlo said.

The other man pulled out a horn and blew it three times. As if in response, an arrow flew through the air and pierced him in the neck. He dropped the horn and fell to the ground.

At that moment Rummy emerged from the infirmary door. When he saw Xan, he took a step toward him but then seemed to rethink his plan. He spit at Xan's feet, turned on his heels, and ran down the cobblestone path, away from the incoming hooves.

Rummy had escaped just in time. Lord Godfrey's men stormed the cobblestone streets on horseback, swords raised in the air. Several bandits ran in terror beneath the fury of the horses.

One bandit plunged to the path as he fled, a deep wound across his back. His falling body tripped up Carlo's feet, and the leader of the bandits crashed down, his sword flying from his hand.

"God wills it!" Lord Godfrey cried out, covered in shining chain mail upon his white steed. Then he and his men hurtled down the road, slashing and yelling, "God wills it!"

At their shouts, a blinding flash lit his mind. Agony like the strike of a serpent; throbbing that could split a skull in two. Sharp pain from the front of his forehead to the back of his neck. Twisting and crushing and grinding his brain to bits.

Memories—so many memories. Maybe everything he'd ever done; ever seen; ever heard. Just like that monk the prior had known. Mother and Father; Hardonbury; the East Field. His true name: Stephen. Everything, as if God Himself had seared the images back into his brain with a firebrand.

Dazed, he stumbled into the path of a mounted guard, still shouting and chasing at bandits.

"Look out, boy!"

The massive brown horse struck Xan's body as it passed. Its impact sent him reeling backward, tripping over a cobbled stone and cracking his head against the wall of the infirmary.

The last thing he saw was three of Lord Godfrey's guards pouncing upon Carlo and pulling the old bandit to his feet by his gray hair.

"Kill this scum," one of them said.

Then a voice—the prior. "Nay! Do not spill this man's blood on this holy ground!"

Then darkness.

24

Forgiveness

Had it all been a dream? The screams, the Shadow, the monks, the bandits, Lord Godfrey: were they all part of a nightmare that wouldn't end?

He opened his eyes. He lay in the infirmary upon a straw mattress again.

Nay, not a dream. It all had happened. Mother and Father were dead.

I am Stephen, son of Nicholas.

He was nothing but a poor serf who'd spent his life working with Father in the fields of Hardonbury Manor, much like the servants who labored at Harwood Abbey. Of course, he'd had friends in the village, but no other family. Before he was born, his parents had lost his brother and sister to a plague. And though Father had spoken of an uncle in a far-off town, that man hadn't come back to Hardonbury since he'd been a child. Perhaps the uncle was dead, like everyone else.

He was all alone in the world.

"Look, he wakes." The soft voice near his bedside belonged to Brother Andrew, the one who had become like a second father, giving him a new identity and a name: Alexander—Xan.

"Welcome back, child," the prior said, stepping to the bed with relief in his eyes.

"You took a nasty fall," Brother Andrew said. "By Adam, you gave me a dreadful fright."

Of course. The bandits had attacked. Lord Godfrey and his men had arrived just in time.

"What happened to those horrid bandits? Rummy and that Carlo—did the guards kill him?"

The prior shook his head. "Carlo dwells in our confinement cell, with two of his accomplices. Unfortunately, I think the one you call Rummy must have escaped."

"That's a shame," Xan said. "They all deserve to die."

The prior gave a disappointed look. "'Tis not good for you to speak so freely about the killing of human life, boy. Our Lord died for men such as that."

Except the prior hadn't lost his mother to men such as that. Maybe then he'd understand.

"What about the abbot?" Xan said, changing the topic. "Lucy and Lord Godfrey?"

"All are safe, son, thanks to you," Brother Andrew said. "Alas, three of Lord Godfrey's men were killed in the battle, and most of the bandits perished, except for a few who fled."

So, Lord Godfrey had come and saved the abbey, and his men had paid the ultimate price.

"I guess the lord will get Penwood Manor after all. Now that he protects the abbey, I mean."

Brother Andrew grinned. "Quite the opposite. The lord is ashamed his bailiff caused such tragedy to us. Indeed, yesterday he gave up all claim to Penwood to atone for Sire Roger's sins."

"Yesterday?"

"Aye, son. You have slept a full day away. We were starting to worry again."

Xan yawned wide and sat up in the bed. "I know who I am," he said in a whisper.

The two monks exchanged concerned glances. "You can remember again?" the prior asked, his face drawn up in an anxious frown.

He nodded. "All the memories hit me at once, just like the monk at your old abbey."

"Very good, child," the prior said. "The abbot will be cheered by this news."

"Wait—what about Brother Leo? We have to get him out of jail!"

"'Tis done already," assured Brother Andrew. "And the abbot has confirmed what you have already told us: Brother Leo was innocent this entire time."

How close they'd come to hanging that poor monk for a crime he'd never committed. The only offense he'd done was being grumpy and walking around the abbey at odd hours with his cowl over his head, terrifying little boys who mistook him for the angel of death.

"There's one thing I still don't understand, Brother. Why was Brother Leo always wandering about like that at night? 'Twas so creepy and suspicious."

Brother Andrew looked to the prior, who gave him a nod. "You may tell him."

"It seems," Brother Andrew said, "that the abbot gave special permission to Brother Leo to engage in . . . well, to discipline himself with a whipping rod upon his own back."

That sounded terrible! The old monk had talked several times about beating his body to make it his slave, but that had always sounded like a mere expression.

Brother Andrew was still explaining. "That is why Brother Leo went to distant areas, where no one would hear him cry out. And that is why you boys saw him sneaking about at odd hours."

"And that's probably why he was limping in pain. But *why* hurt himself like that, Brother?"

"'Tis a dangerous form of penance to share Christ's sufferings," the prior said. "He wished to keep it a secret. That kind of self-punishment requires special permission from the abbot. Indeed, Leo did have his approval, but I did not know about that 'til the abbot awoke yesterday."

Xan lay back, already exhausted from the brief conversation.

A woman's melody rang in from the hallway. "Praise God! See who's awake, Lucy!" Sister Regina and Lucy entered the room, escorted by Brother Lucius. The nun greeted the monks and squeezed the boy's hand. "We have all been praying for you."

Lucy folded her arms and put on a pretend pout. "You're always causing people to worry. Why must you fall down all the time?"

Sister Regina's gentle laugh at Lucy's joke sounded a lot like Mother. She too had been kind and loving, humming songs at night while he went to sleep. Father had especially loved those songs.

But Xan—Stephen—would never hear either of their dear voices again now, thanks to Sire Roger and Rummy and the leader of that evil group of bandits, Carlo.

The abbot trudged in front of them into the confinement building, a cane in one hand and a monk's supporting arm in the other. Each step caused a grunt of pain from the injured monk.

"Now you watch and listen, child," the abbot said, turning toward him. "Listen with your whole heart and soul. This may bring you healing; help you see the value in every human life."

But how could watching the abbot speak to that evil man bring healing? The only place he wanted to see Carlo was at the end of the hangman's noose, if they allowed boys to watch.

Hopefully Lord Godfrey and the royal courts would take care of that soon enough.

Brother Andrew had insisted that they walk together behind the abbot and watch the old monk speak to the man who had attacked him and almost killed him.

Carlo apparently had been talking freely to Lord Godfrey's guards, who now kept watch over the captured bandits in the abbey's confinement cells. According to Brother Andrew, the bandit had been without remorse for his crimes. Indeed, the only sorrow he seemed to feel was for the injury to his shoulder, inflicted by Godfrey's men when they'd transported him to the cell.

He'd told the guards all they'd wanted to know, seeing no reason to hide the truth. He'd confessed that he had been hired by Sire Roger to cause havoc in the countryside. That had been no problem for him and his bandits. Not only were they permitted to take whatever they found, but the bailiff had paid them handsomely for their services.

He'd attacked Hardonbury. Then he'd assailed Penwood and the abbey. When that hadn't satisfied Sire Roger, Carlo had disguised himself in the robe of a monk to inflict a beating on the stubborn old abbot so the abbey would have no choice but to seek Lord Godfrey's protection.

Yet Sire Roger now rotted in Lord Godfrey's dungeon, and Carlo was caged like an animal, while the abbot walked free and the abbey was given undisputed ownership of Penwood Manor. God truly could bring good out of evil, just as Sister Regina had said.

The abbey's confinement area was tiny and dank, with three rooms, each containing a jail cell. The other two captured bandits had been separated from Carlo and kept in different cells.

As the abbot entered the room that held Carlo, Brother Andrew put his hand out. "Stay with me here, my son," he said. "We can see and hear all that we need without getting too close."

Once, back in Hardonbury, Father had stopped him from going into the shed because of a serpent. "Stay here, Stephen," Father had said. "Do not get too close to that perilous creature."

Carlo was like a serpent, too—a poisonous one.

A guard met the monk at the doorway. "You are walking again already, abbot?"

The abbot began a chuckle that ended in a cough. "I just thank God to be alive, friend." He plodded toward the cell that contained Carlo, then sat in a small chair there. He made the Sign of the Cross with his thick, muscular hands.

Carlo seemed provoked by the mere presence of the holy monk. "Why come here to torment me, old man? I suppose you want to gloat."

"You are the one who attacked me?" the abbot asked, his weak voice barely a whisper.

The bandit smiled thinly. "They told you about me, eh?"

The abbot said nothing as he watched Carlo, but the bandit couldn't bear his gaze for long. He soon turned his eyes to the ground, which was a good thing—the villain didn't deserve to look into the face of a good man like the abbot.

"Do not worry, Abbot. I shall be hanged for my crimes. You soon will be satisfied."

The abbot shook his head. "There will be no satisfaction in your death."

Perhaps the abbot wouldn't be happy when the bandit was executed, but others would. The entire village of Hardonbury would probably line up and take turns walking all over his grave.

Carlo laughed aloud. "Come now, old man. We both know you will spit on my tomb."

"Nay. Indeed, I have spoken to Lord Godfrey on your behalf. You will not be executed."

"What?"

The abbot must be jesting. How could he intervene on behalf of a vile man who had wanted to kill him, who had burned the abbey, who had even murdered women and children?! Mother and Father were in their graves because of him.

"God gave you life," the abbot said. "Only God shall take it from you."

Carlo seemed dazed. "But the penalty for my crimes is death. Others will demand it."

"They shall respect my wishes. You will not be executed," the abbot repeated.

Brother Andrew's face had stayed expressionless through this part of the conversation. Had he known what the abbot had done? Surely he couldn't approve of this, allowing a killer to live.

"I will not be hung?" Carlo muttered to himself. Then he grinned, as though he'd figured out the true motive behind the abbot's actions. "I see, old man. You wish me to suffer in a dungeon the rest of my days. That would be a fate worse than death, eh?"

"Nay, that is not what I desire. I wish to forgive you for your sin against me."

The abbot reached his hand through the bars, as if to touch Carlo's shoulder. That seemed dangerous. A man like Carlo, with nothing to lose, might grab his arm and break it to pieces.

But Carlo didn't grab the abbot's arm. Instead, he stepped back and turned his head away. "I did not ask for your forgiveness. Nor do I need it."

The abbot waited. "Perhaps so," he said finally. "But *I* need to forgive *you*. Our Lord forgave those who crucified him, and He has forgiven my own selfish sins. So now I forgive you."

Carlo remained silent.

Why would God want to forgive someone who had done so much evil? Carlo was exactly the kind of person who deserved to be punished forever, wasn't he? In Hardonbury, there used to live a bullying boy named Thomas, who'd punched Xan in the mouth once for no good reason. When Thomas's parents found out, they'd beat him with a plank twenty times. Surely all the crimes Carlo had committed deserved much more punishment and much less forgiveness.

When Carlo spoke next, his voice sounded sad. "There is no forgiveness for me. Go away."

The abbot regarded Carlo for a long moment, as though examining his soul through the bandit's black eyes. Whatever he saw, he didn't talk about it.

"As you wish," the abbot said, rising feebly from the chair.

That whole conversation had been odd. If Brother Leo had been here, he would probably have pointed his stubby finger in the bandit's face and doomed him to hell.

"Come," Brother Andrew said, tugging at his tunic sleeve.

But as the abbot reached the doorway, the bandit stirred.

"Wait!" Carlo called. His proud head was hung low; his defiant posture had vanished; the angry fire in his eyes had faded. He looked beaten on the inside.

The abbot gave a nod to the bandit and shuffled back over to the bars of his cell.

"I was not always as you see me now," Carlo said in a softer tone. "I took up the cross and fought in Bernard's Crusade when I was a young man—a dreamer—journeying back to England after visiting relatives in Sicily. As I traveled through France, I heard Bernard of Clairvaux preaching his crusade. I was much taken by him, so I followed."

Just like Lord Godfrey's father and Sire Roger's father, Carlo too had been a crusader. Carlo must have felt like a real devil when he'd heard Lord Godfrey's men shouting out the crusader's war cry as he was about to kill an innocent boy.

The abbot again reached through the bars. "'Tis not too late for you."

This time, Carlo didn't pull back. "What must I do?"

"Be sorry for your sins, confess them, and receive God's forgiveness," the abbot said. "Then go and sin no more."

Carlo remained still, his chin dropped to his chest.

"I am a priest," the abbot said. "I will hear you in Confession, if you wish. With that sacrament will come healing."

Brother Andrew pulled him to the front door. "We must go now, my son," he said firmly, leaving no room for discussion. In a moment, they were blinking back in the sunlight.

"The abbot is going to forgive him, Brother?" he said. "Give him Confession? You mean, Carlo might get into Heaven one day, even after all the evil he's done?"

Brother Andrew shrugged. "'Tis a mystery, son. The abbot is a holy man, and our Lord wants us to forgive. All of us have sinned and deserve eternal death, yet He came to offer us life."

Xan stepped away from the monk. "He killed my parents. How can anyone forgive him for that? 'Tis impossible."

Brother Andrew put a hand on the boy's shoulder. "With God, all things are possible. Pray, son. Pray and let God heal you. Give it time, and you will see."

He shook his head. "That villain doesn't deserve forgiveness. Not now."

Maybe not ever.

Epilogue

He stood with Brother Andrew over his parents' graves. The names "Nicholas" and "Helen" were carved on the wooden crosses, but their faces would survive only in his memories.

The monk made the Sign of the Cross. "May perpetual light shine upon these dear souls."

His parents were gone forever now. He'd solved the mystery of their deaths, but now he remembered how much he missed their lives. A warm wetness raced down his cheeks.

Maybe it was all right to mourn. So much evil had befallen him and his family and his village and this abbey. And Brother Andrew had said that mourning would bring healing, perhaps even forgiveness for those vile bandits one day.

His tears slowed and then stopped. Brother Andrew embraced him warmly. "You will have a home with us for as long as you desire it—Stephen."

Saint Stephen had been a man of faith, but he'd been martyred. Maybe Stephen must become a martyr again. Indeed, maybe Stephen's life was over.

"I'm sorry, Brother," he said. "Stephen's life can't be saved."

The monk seemed startled. "Nay, son. God still has a purpose for your life."

He shook his head. "You misunderstand, Brother. Remember how you said your real name, Robert, died the day you took your vows? Well, Stephen died the day I came to this abbey."

The name of Stephen would be forever buried in those graves with Mother and Father.

Brother Andrew's blue eye regained its glimmer. "I see. Well then, let's go home—Xan."

A smile formed on the edges of the boy's lips. Maybe he *had* found his home. And his identity.

I am Xan.

Author's Historical Note

Although the characters and events in *Shadow in the Dark* are fictional, the novel takes place in a historical place and time. The story is set in medieval England in A.D. 1184, during the final years of the reign of King Henry II (1153–1189). Xan, the main character, is a peasant boy growing up in a remote part of the country.

Kings, Manors, and Serfs

More than a century before Xan was born—in 1066—his nation had gone through a revolutionary transformation when William the Conqueror crossed the English Channel and invaded England from Normandy, an area of Northern France populated by descendants of the Vikings ("the Northmen" or "Normans").

After the Conquest, King William constructed many castles and cathedrals in England and gave large estates and manor houses to wealthy Normans who were loyal to him. When *Shadow in the Dark* took place, English society was still a feudal system, also called "the manorial system." Most of European society was set up this way during the Middle Ages.

In this system, people such as Xan's parents were peasant "serfs" who lived and worked on the land of a manor. They were at the bottom rung of the English social ladder. All the lands still belonged to the king, who was lord over all English lands, but the king redistributed ownership to his loyalists, who were called land barons. These land barons further divided their lands into manors. In charge of the manors were lesser landlords and knights, all of whom had to serve the king when duty called. Peasants like Xan and his family were allowed to live on manor lands as long as they paid rent and provided labor for their landlords.

Abbeys, Monks, Novices, and Lay Brothers

The injured Xan ended up at Harwood Abbey, a Benedictine monastery. Monks of this religious order lived according to the Rule of Saint Benedict, which organized a life of prayer and work. The abbey was ruled by an abbot; next in charge was the prior. Many of the men at an abbey would be monks who had already taken vows and belonged to the Benedictine order. But there would be novices also, who were training to be monks and still deciding if this was the right life for them. A man might become a novice as an adult, but often the novices were young, just teenagers. Men who worked at the abbey but who were not monks were called lay brothers, and there were also servants who helped with the work. Benedictine monks were sometimes called "black monks" because they wore simple black robes.

Harwood Abbey of *Shadow in the Dark* has a monastery of Benedictine monks and also, a short distance away, a convent of Benedictine nuns. The monks and nuns at Harwood Abbey spend most of their time praying, working, and copying manuscripts. Benedictine monks and nuns (and the Church itself) played a major role in preserving written works of the ancient Greeks and Romans, along with the Sacred Scriptures (the Bible). As Xan becomes accustomed to the abbey, he gets a taste of life in a medieval monastery. He sees that the abbey and convent each have one person in charge—the abbot or abbess—along with their assistants, such as priors and obedientiaries. Xan sees the monks gathering to pray in the abbey church seven times throughout the day and night. He participates in some of their meetings in the chapter house, where they conduct abbey business. He learns about writing and works with the ink and goat parchment used to copy manuscripts.

Children in Medieval Times

In some ways, children during the Middle Ages were like children of any period. Their parents loved and cared for them, they enjoyed toys and games, they were taught to help around the home, and they liked making friends with other children. In other ways, medieval children had quite a different life from many children today. Only children from wealthy families could expect a school education. And once they reached puberty—ages 12 to 14—they were considered adults. Peasant children helped with household work or in the fields; some moved away to work as servants on other estates. Boys from wealthy families might be sent away to be trained as knights, and the girls would receive the kind of training to prepare them to be proper ladies with their own households. They tended to get married much earlier than we do today, often during their early teens, which meant that they became parents early, too.

The Middle Ages happened centuries before societies thought much about equality. No one expected to work their way up to a better place on the social ladder. The peasant knew that he had little power and that the rich man whose estate he worked on had a lot of power—this was simply the way things were.

Also, men had a more prominent role in society than women. Even a girl whose parents were wealthy did not have many choices about her own life. Her father could choose her husband, and then her husband's decisions would rule their household. A girl's options were quite limited, whether she was rich or poor. She might marry and have a family—or she might join a religious order and dedicate her life to God's service. In Xan's story, his friend Lucy is not a peasant, as Xan is; her father is a minor nobleman, which means that Lucy has some advantages and opportunities. Yet, at her young age she is considering becoming a nun. For her time, it is not unusual for a girl such as Lucy to consider the religious life before she's even a teenager.

In *Shadow in the Dark*, a group of orphans lives at Harwood Abbey. This was not a typical situation, but it's not surprising that the monks and nuns would provide a safe place for children if needed. However, it would be common for there to be novice boys whose families brought them to abbeys to be trained to become monks. Xan observes some of the novices at Harwood Abbey and realizes that one potential path for his future is to become a novice himself.

Glossary

abbey Another term for monastery, where monks and priests live in community

abbot The superior of an abbey

Bernard of Clairvaux French abbot (1090–1153) who became well known for his mystical writings. He became a saint and was named a Doctor of the Church.

chain mail A type of armor made of metal links

chapter house A building attached to a monastery or a cathedral in which meetings are held and business addressed

compline Part of the Liturgy of the Hours, the public prayer of the Church to praise God and sanctify the day. Also known as Night Prayer, *compline* is the final prayer of the day, said before bedtime.

Crusades A series of medieval military campaigns between Christians and Muslims for control of sites in the Holy Land

granges Another term for farmlands

infirmary A place where sick or injured people receive treatment and care

land baron A nobleman who was given a title and land in exchange for pledging allegiance to the king

lettered Formally educated

mace A heavy club with metal spikes used in the Middle Ages

Moors The term used in medieval times to refer to Muslims who lived in what is now Spain, Portugal, and North Africa. In the Crusades, the Christians and the Moors fought for control of the Holy Land.

narthex The lobby area leading into a medieval cathedral

nocturns The term for the three division in Matins, the prayer said during the night in the Liturgy of the Hours

nones The midafternoon prayer in the Liturgy of the Hours, the public prayer of the Church to praise God and sanctify the day. *Nones* are prayed at approximately 3 p.m.

novice A monk in training who has not yet taken final vows. The purpose of the novitiate period is to determine if the novice is truly called to the religious life.

obedientiary A lesser official in a medieval monastery who reports to the abbot and the prior

prime The morning prayer in Liturgy of the Hours, the public prayer of the Church to praise God and sanctify the day. *Prime* is prayed at approximately 6 a.m.

prior The person in charge of the abbey after the abbot

quarrel The arrow designed for a crossbow

refectory The dining room of a monastery

Saint Benedict The founder of the Benedictine Order (A.D. 480–547)

scriptorium a room, often in a monastery, where Scripture and other important books were copied by hand

seal A symbol imprinted in hot wax used to seal a document. The imprint identifies the sender of the document, and the intact seal provides proof that the document has not been opened by anyone else.

sext The midday prayer in the Liturgy of the Hours, the public prayer of the Church to praise God and sanctify the day. It is prayed at approximately noon.

shire A county or similar division of land

terce The midmorning prayer in the Liturgy of the Hours, the public prayer of the Church to praise God and sanctify the day. It is prayed at approximately 9 a.m.

The Rule The book written by Benedict in 516 of the rules and concepts for how a monastic community should live. *The Rule* addressed spiritual and practical matters and helped shape how religious orders were organized and operated.

whipping rod A small whip that a person would use to strike himself or herself on the back as a form of voluntary penance, considered a way to discipline the physical body for spiritual benefit. This practice, also called flagellation, was condemned by Pope Clement VI in 1349 because of widespread abuses.

Acknowledgments

I hope you were blessed and enriched by experiencing Xan's story in *Shadow in the Dark*. But this novel was not the product of my efforts alone. Indeed, it would not exist without the hard work of many others, for whom I am deeply thankful to God. I regret having space to mention only a few of those names here.

First, I greatly appreciate the love and support of my family, especially my wife, Alisa, and my son, A.J., who both inspired me, suggested many great ideas, and became invaluable sounding boards for the series. The idea for these novels sprang from one of my family's cross-country road trips during a change in military assignments. We spoke at length in the car about ideas for an exciting book that would engage today's youth while also grappling with issues of the moral and religious life. From that conversation emerged the concept of *Shadow in the Dark*, including the character of Xan, the location of Harwood Abbey, and the mysterious "Shadow" lurking at the abbey.

Second, I am grateful for the generous advice and consultation of Dr. Jennifer Paxton, a professor in the Department of History at the Catholic University of America, Washington, D.C. An expert in twelfth-century English abbeys, Dr. Paxton helped me conform Xan's world ever closer to the historical reality of that period.

Third, I owe a very large debt of gratitude for the prayers and kind advice of other authors who took the time to review my book, especially those in the Catholic Writers Guild, as well as for the mentorship of Ramona Tucker and Jeff Nesbit, who were the first professionals to truly believe in my writing.

Finally, I am so grateful for the dedication of the entire staff at Loyola Press, who have taken this novel and raised it to the next level through their professionalism and investment in the series. Their incredible team—with a special shout-out to Jim Thomas and Tim Travaglini—helped make innumerable improvements to this story and to my writing. Special thanks to Joseph Durepos, Joellyn Cicciarelli, Maria Cuadrado, Vinita Wright, Carrie Freyer, Andrew Yankech, and Mandy Lemos. And to the many, many others who have personally worked on making this book a success. I owe you all a great debt.

For those who have read this novel, I pray it has been a blessing to you, and I hope you will keep reading the series. There is much more to come in the adventures of Xan and Lucy!

About the Author

Antony Barone Kolenc retired as a Lieutenant Colonel from the U.S. Air Force Judge Advocate General's Corps after 21 years of military service. He is a law professor who teaches courses on constitutional and military law and has been published in numerous journals and magazines, and he speaks at legal, writing, and home education events. He and his wife, Alisa, have raised five children and are proud of their three beautiful grandchildren.